WALL·E

This book belongs to

..................................

..................................

This edition published by Parragon in 2011
Parragon
Queen Street House
4 Queen Street
Bath BA1 1HE, UK



ISBN 978-1-4454-4021-7

Printed in China

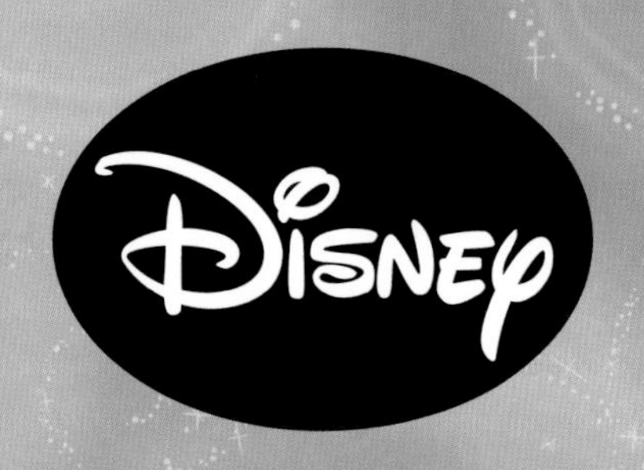

# Contents

43
43
43
95
TWIN H-
PISTON
CUP

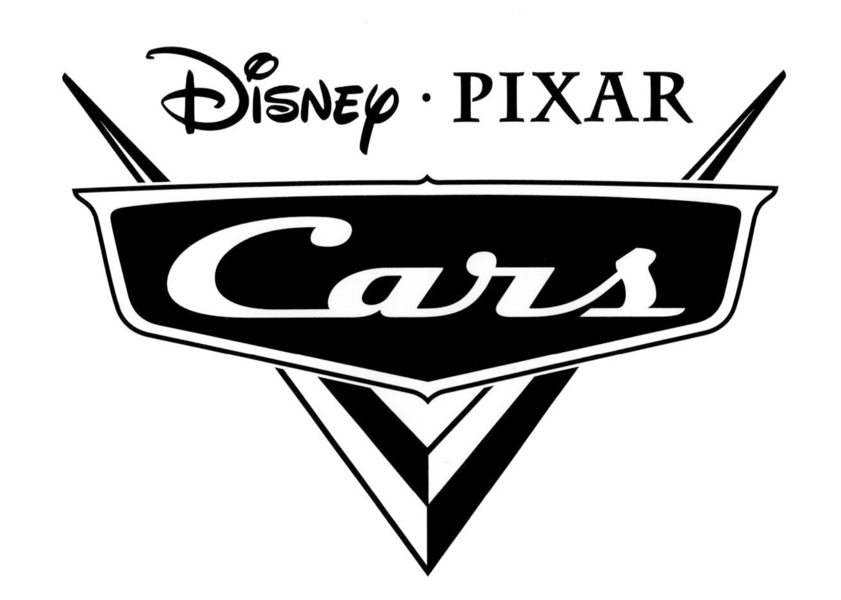
Disney · PIXAR
Cars

STARRING

LIGHTNING McQUEEN

SALLY

MATER

CHICK HICKS

DOC

Disney · PIXAR
Cars

"Pit stop! Pit stop!" cried Guido as he zoomed over and joined the gang at Flo's café.

The little forklift buzzed with excitement. Would his friend Lightning McQueen win the Piston Cup?

Earlier that week, Lightning had accidentally found himself in Radiator Springs on his way to the tie-breaker race in California. He had to work hard in Radiator Springs, but he also made lots of friends. Now, everyone in Radiator Springs was sad that Lightning was gone . . . but also excited about his big race.

“Do you think he can beat Chick Hicks?” wondered Sally. “I hear Chick is one mean racecar.”

“Lightning can beat anybody, I know it!” said Mater. Lightning and Mater had become best friends in a very short time.

Mater believed in Lightning, one hundred percent!

PISTON
CUP
CHICK HICKS
CHAMPION
htB
htB

They watched a car with a bright green paint job fill the TV screen. It was Lightning McQueen's rival, Chick Hicks!

"Lightning? Why should I worry about him?" Chick's voice came through the TV speaker. "He ended up in some rusty little town, playing with tractors and taking Sunday drives. He's not serious about winning. But I am!"

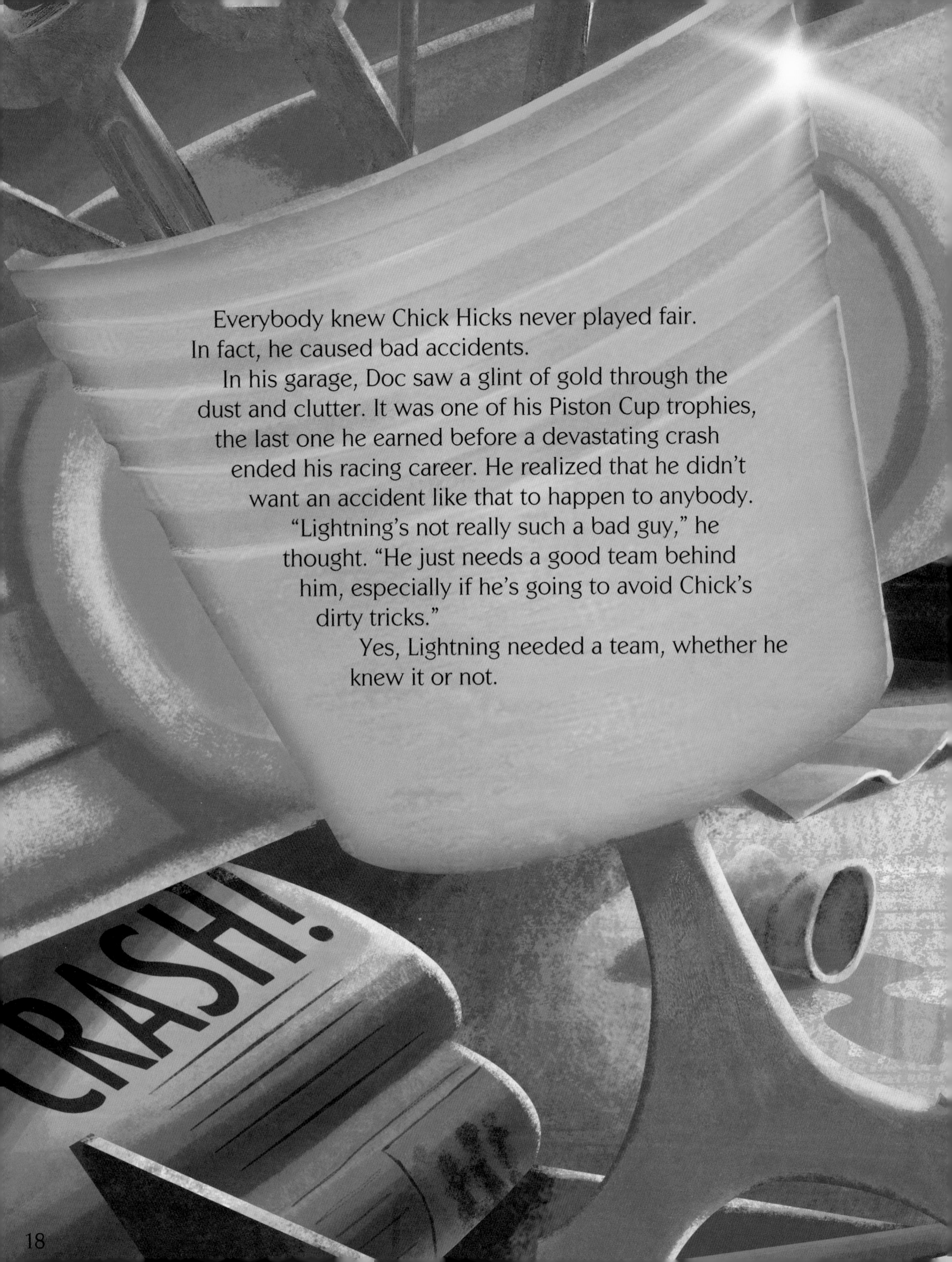


Everybody knew Chick Hicks never played fair. In fact, he caused bad accidents.

In his garage, Doc saw a glint of gold through the dust and clutter. It was one of his Piston Cup trophies, the last one he earned before a devastating crash ended his racing career. He realized that he didn't want an accident like that to happen to anybody.

"Lightning's not really such a bad guy," he thought. "He just needs a good team behind him, especially if he's going to avoid Chick's dirty tricks."

Yes, Lightning needed a team, whether he knew it or not.

"Listen up, everybody," Doc's voice boomed down the main street from Flo's all the way to Sally's motel. "The rookie needs our help. He's out there with no pit crew and two tough opponents. I'm not going to let Lightning McQueen lose just because he thinks he can do it all on his own. Who's with me?"

Everybody was, of course!

Luigi and Guido got to work choosing some tyres. Lightning McQueen would need some good ones.

By morning the crew was inside the stadium. What a feeling it was, to be surrounded by all that excitement! But the Radiator Springs crew had a job to do.

"Pit stop!" said Guido when he saw all the pitties and their tool racks. As soon as Mater unhooked him, he rolled over to a spot to set up.

Sarge took command when he saw the orderly layout of the pit lane and the precise actions of the racing teams.

"You, Flo, over here," he ordered. "Guido, we need the tyres right there."

Ramone had something else in mind, "Hey, Doc! Let me give you a paint job. You gotta let these folks know that you're an important car".

"Not me," said Doc. "Try snazzing-up this pit instead. We need to show off our star car, not me."

Doc drove over to the other side of the track to check out the other crews. But as he neared Chick Hicks' tent he overheard something bad – really bad.

“I’m not gonna let anyone get in the way of me winning that race today,” Chick said to his crew. “If I have to, I’ll make The King and that rookie wipe out so fast their tyres won’t even spin.”

Doc peeked in and saw Chick turn and wink to his crew. “The Cup is mine, boys,” said Chick.

Doc felt his oil heat up. He couldn’t stand for this! It was time to help Lightning, even if it took his last drop of fuel. Could he find Lightning in time to warn him about Chick’s evil plans? Doc returned so fast to the group that he almost overheated.

"This is what friendship is all about," thought Doc as Ramone finished painting him. "We are all a family."

And then, as a high-octane boost rushed through him, he climbed the crew-chief platform – with Ramone's blazing letters freshly painted on his side: Number 51, The Fabulous Hudson Hornet.

FABULOUS HUDSON
HORNET
51

"Look, it's the Hudson Hornet!" cried a car in the stands.

The crowd roared and cheered, louder and louder. Everywhere, Doc saw a sea of flashing headlights and flying antenna balls. They were cheering for him!

Doc was too focused on the upcoming race to smile. But it was clear – Doc Hudson was proud to be back, and it felt good to hear the crowds roaring their approval.

43
95
TWIN H
PISTON
CUP

It was all so exciting that no one in the crowd really cared when Chick Hicks was announced the winner of the tiebreaker race.

Instead, they cheered for Lightning as he helped The King cross the finish line. They cheered as they watched Lightning cruise on over to his crew chief, Doc, the Hudson Hornet.

Yes, indeed, the crowd cheered for the real winners of this race: Lightning McQueen and his Radiator Springs family.

Back in Radiator Springs, everybody gathered at Flo's to hear about the race.

"Doc and I want to build a racing headquarters near the town," Lightning told Sally.

Doc nodded. "It will be a special design – a first-class track that won't spoil our beautiful desert landscape."

"A great idea," said Sally.

"And it will put Radiator Springs back on the map."

Rust-eze

It wasn't long before Radiator Springs became an international racing sensation. Doc and Lightning sent invitations to race cars all over the world. They came to the town to share tips and techniques on how to become better racers.

THE END

Disney
fairies
TinkerBell

TINKER BELL

VIDIA

STARRING

IRIDESSA

ROSETTA

QUEEN CLARION

Disney
fairies
TinkerBell

One winter's day in London, a baby laughed for the very first time. That laugh floated up and away to meet its destiny. It would become a fairy, just like all first laughs.

It flew straight for the Second Star to the Right, and passed through it in a burst of light. On the other side was . . . Never Land!

The laugh floated towards a magical place in the heart of the island. This was Pixie Hollow, home of the fairies!

Vidia, the fastest flying fairy of them all, guided the arrival into the Pixie Dust Tree. There, a dust-keeper named Terence sprinkled it with pixie dust, and it took the shape of a tiny, adorable fairy.

Clarion, queen of the fairies, helped the newcomer unfurl her two gossamer wings. The new fairy flapped her wings and realized she could fly!

Queen Clarion waved her hand, and several toadstools sprung up around the Pixie Dust Well. Fairies immediately fluttered forwards to place different objects on the pedestals. Rosetta, a garden fairy, brought a flower. Silvermist, a water fairy, carried a droplet of water. Iridessa, a light fairy, placed a lamp on her pedestal.

"They will help you find your talent," the queen explained to the new fairy.

The youngster timidly placed her hand on a beautiful flower. Its glow instantly faded. She reached for a water droplet, but that, too, faded.

The fairy moved on without touching anything else – she was afraid to fail again – but then something amazing happened. As she passed by a hammer, it began to glow. Then it rose up off its pedestal and flew straight for her!

"I've never seen one glow that much before," said Silvermist.

"I do believe you're right," agreed Rosetta. "Li'l daisy-top might be a very rare talent indeed!"

Vidia glowered. She had one of the strongest and rarest talents in Pixie Hollow, and she wasn't looking for competition.

"Tinker fairies," called the queen. "Welcome the newest member of your talent guild – Tinker Bell!"

A large fairy named Clank and a bespectacled fairy named Bobble came forwards to greet Tink. Then they whisked her off for a flying tour of Pixie Hollow. It was almost time for the changing of the seasons, and they could see everyone getting ready.

Finally, the trio landed at Tinkers' Nook. Tink looked around and saw fairies fixing and fashioning all kinds of amazing, useful objects.

Next Clank and Bobble took Tinker Bell to her own little house, which had a closet filled with clothes. The garments turned out to be much too big, but Tink knew just how to fix them.

Tinker Bell put on her new dress and tied her hair up. Then she reported to the workshop. Clank and Bobble couldn't wait to show her all the handy things that tinker fairies made.

Soon Fairy Mary – the no-nonsense fairy who ran Tinkers' Nook – arrived. She noticed the new fairy's dainty hands. "Don't worry, dear, we'll build up those tinker muscles in no time," she exclaimed.

Then, after reminding Clank and Bobble to make their deliveries, she was gone.

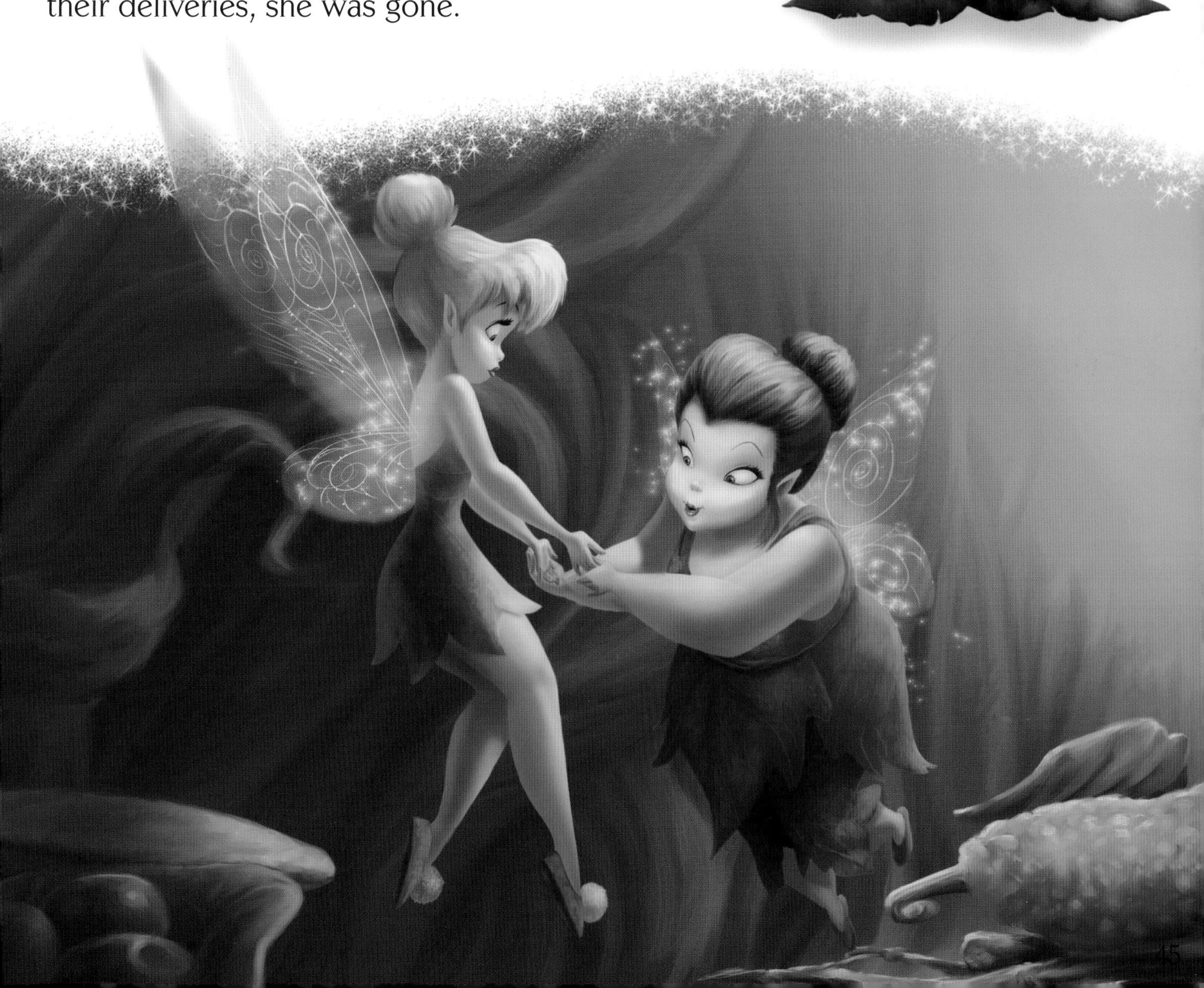

A little while later, Tink, Clank and Bobble were on their way. Luckily they had Cheese the mouse – and Clank – to pull the loaded wagon.

PITTER-PATTER! PITTER-PATTER!

The friends heard a sound behind them.

"Sprinting Thistles! Aaaaagh!" screamed Clank. The weeds nearby had come to life and were headed straight for them! The wagon pitched this way and that. Then it lurched down the path and landed in a flowerbed in Springtime Square.

Rosetta, Silvermist, Iridessa and Fawn rushed over to help their friends. The tinkers were unhurt, and soon ready to go back to their deliveries. There were rainbow tubes for Iridessa, milkweed-pod satchels for Fawn and pussy-willow brushes for Rosetta.

Iridessa explained that she would roll up rainbows, put them in the tubes, and take them to the mainland.

"What's the mainland?" Tink asked.

"It's where we're going to go for spring, to change the seasons," replied Silvermist.

Next the tinkers stopped at the Flower Meadow, where Vidia was vacuuming the pollen out of flowers with her whirlwind.

Tinker Bell startled Vidia, and the just-filled pots fell over.

"Hi! What's your talent?" Tink asked.

"I am a fast-flying fairy. Fairies of every talent depend on me," answered Vidia. She made it clear that she didn't think much of tinker fairies.

Tink was insulted. "When I go to the mainland, I'll prove just how important we are!" she replied.

Tink flew off, grumbling to herself. Soon, however, something down on the beach caught her attention. When she landed, she discovered several wonderful treasures buried in the sand.

"Lost Things," said Clank when Tink brought her finds to the Tinkers' Nook workshop.

"They wash up on Never Land from time to time," explained Bobble.

Fairy Mary whisked the trinkets away. The queen's review of the springtime preparations was that night, and there was a lot to do.

Tink decided this was her chance to prove to Vidia just how important a tinker's talent really was!

That evening, the Minister of Spring welcomed Queen Clarion to the review ceremony.

"I think you'll find we have things well in hand," he said proudly. "When the Everblossom blooms, we will be ready to bring spring to the mainland."

Suddenly, Tinker Bell interrupted the proceedings. "I came up with some fantastic things for tinkers to use when we go to the mainland!" she told the queen excitedly.

Tink pulled a homemade paint sprayer out of the wagon and demonstrated it on a flower that needed coloring. But instead of spraying paint, it exploded.

"Has no one explained?" Queen Clarion said gently. "Tinker fairies don't go to the mainland. All of those things are done by the nature-talent fairies. I'm sorry."

The next morning, Tink asked her friends to teach her how to be a nature fairy. She really wanted to go to the mainland. Reluctantly, the other fairies agreed to help. No fairy had ever changed his or her talent before!

Tink's first lesson was on how to become a water fairy. Silvermist showed her how to place a dewdrop on a spider's web, but each time Tink tried, the dewdrop burst.

The light-fairy lesson didn't go any better. Tink lost control of the light and attracted a group of fireflies. They thought Tink's glow was irresistible!

Fawn had Tink's animal fairy lesson all planned. "We're teaching baby birds how to fly," she announced.

Fawn went to a nest, smiled at a bird, and gently encouraged it until the fluffy little creature was flying along right behind her.

Unfortunately, Tink's baby bird seemed terrified. When she nudged it towards the edge of the nest, it even tried to fight her!

"If I end up making acorn kettles the rest of my life, I am holding you personally responsible," Tinker Bell said impatiently.

Tink looked up and saw a majestic bird soaring in the sky. She decided she would ask it to help her teach the baby bird.

Suddenly an ear-splitting screech filled the forest. The bird was a hawk!

Tink hurtled down into the knothole of a tree – but Vidia was already hiding there. Soon the hawk discovered them both, so they jumped down a tunnel inside the tree. When Vidia reached the end of the chute, she could see the hawk outside. She stopped in the nick of time – but Tink accidentally slammed into her and sent Vidia shooting out of the tree. The hawk opened its beak, ready to strike. Luckily, the other fairies were able to chase the bird off.

Vidia was furious. Tink felt awful.

A little while later, Tinker Bell sat on the beach. "Great," she muttered. "At this rate, I should get to the mainland right about, oh, never!"

She angrily threw a pebble and heard a CLUNK! Tink went to investigate and found a broken porcelain box.

By the time her friends found her, Tinker Bell was busily putting her discovery back together. The final touch was a lovely porcelain ballerina that fit into the lid. Tinker Bell gave the dancer a spin, and to her delight, the box played music!

"Do you even realize what you're doing?" asked Rosetta. "Fixing stuff like this – that's what tinkering is!"

"Who cares about going to the mainland anyway?" Silvermist added.

Tink realized her friends didn't want her to change talents. Desperate, she went to visit the only fairy she thought might be able to help.

But Vidia was not in the mood for visitors – especially Tinker Bell.

"You're my last hope," pleaded Tink. "Rosetta won't even try to teach me to be a garden fairy now."

That gave Vidia an idea. She suggested that Tinker Bell prove she was a garden fairy by capturing the Sprinting Thistles.

Tink knew this was her last chance to get to go to the mainland. She built a corral and made a lasso. She rode Cheese into Needlepoint Meadow and used twigs to herd a pair of Thistles into the corral.

"It's working!" Tink cried joyfully. But as she headed back out into the meadow, Vidia quietly blew open the corral gate. The two Thistles ran right out.

Soon other Thistles joined the two that had escaped. It was a stampede!

"Wait! Come back!" yelled Tinker Bell, riding after them.

The Thistles headed to Springtime Square, where they trampled over the carefully organized springtime supplies.

Just then, Queen Clarion appeared. A look of shock crossed her face. "By the Second Star . . . all the preparations for spring – !"

"I'm sorry," Tink whispered as she took to the sky.

Tink decided to leave Pixie Hollow forever, but she couldn't go without one last visit to the workshop. She had to admit that she did love to tinker.

At the workshop, she noticed Cheese sniffing around something at the back of the room – it was trinkets Fairy Mary had taken from her on her first day in Pixie Hollow.

"Lost Things . . . that's it!" she cried as she took them over to her worktable. Tink thought she had an idea that would fix everything.

That night, Queen Clarion gathered all the fairies and explained that spring would not come that year. There simply wasn't enough time to replace all the supplies that had been ruined.

"Wait!" Tinker Bell cried. "I know how we can fix everything!" The clever fairy had designed speedy machines to fix what the Thistles had trampled. She had even used Lost Things to repair her paint sprayer.

Vidia was furious. "Corral the Thistles . . ." she muttered, "I should have told you to go after the hawk!"

Queen Clarion heard this, and looked sharply at Vidia. "I think your fast-flying talent is well-suited to chasing down each and every one of the Thistles," she said sternly.

Tink showed a group of fairies how to assemble a machine to make berry paint. Next she rigged up a vacuum that could collect huge amounts of seeds at a time.

The fairies worked all night using Tink's machines. Early the next morning, Queen Clarion and the ministers of the seasons flew into the square. Before them were more springtime supplies than they had ever seen!

The sun rose, and the Everblossom opened and gave off a golden glow, signaling that it was time to bring springtime to the world. The fairies cheered.

"You did it, Tinker Bell," congratulated Queen Clarion.

"We all did it," Tink replied.

"Queen Clarion," said Silvermist. "Can't Tink come with us to the mainland?"

"It's okay," Tink protested. "My work is here."

Fairy Mary flew over, looking sternly at Tink. "I don't think so, missy!" she said.

She gave a little whistle, and Clank and Bobble led in the wagon. Tink's music box was inside, all polished and shiny.

"I'd imagine there's someone out there who's missing this. Perhaps a certain tinker fairy has a job to do after all . . . on the mainland," said Fairy Mary.

The nature fairies and Tink went to London. They spread out over the city to deliver their springtime magic.

Tinker Bell found the home where the music box belonged, and tapped on the windowpane. A little girl named Wendy Darling poked her head out of the window. Tink watched from her hiding place as Wendy's face filled with happiness at the discovery of her long-lost treasure. The girl took a small key from a chain around her neck and turned it in a slot. The music box began to play!

Soon the fairies' work was done and it was time for them all to return to Never Land. Tink couldn't wait to get home – she had lots of tinkering to do!

THE END

Disney • PIXAR

# TOY STORY

BUZZ
LIGHTYEAR

REX

STARRING

WOODY

SLINKY

HAMM

# Disney • PIXAR

# TOY STORY

Woody the cowboy was Andy's favourite toy. He lived in Andy's bedroom with Slinky Dog, Rex the dinosaur, Mr Potato Head, Hamm the pig, Bo Beep and all the other toys. These toys were special. When no one was around, they came to life!

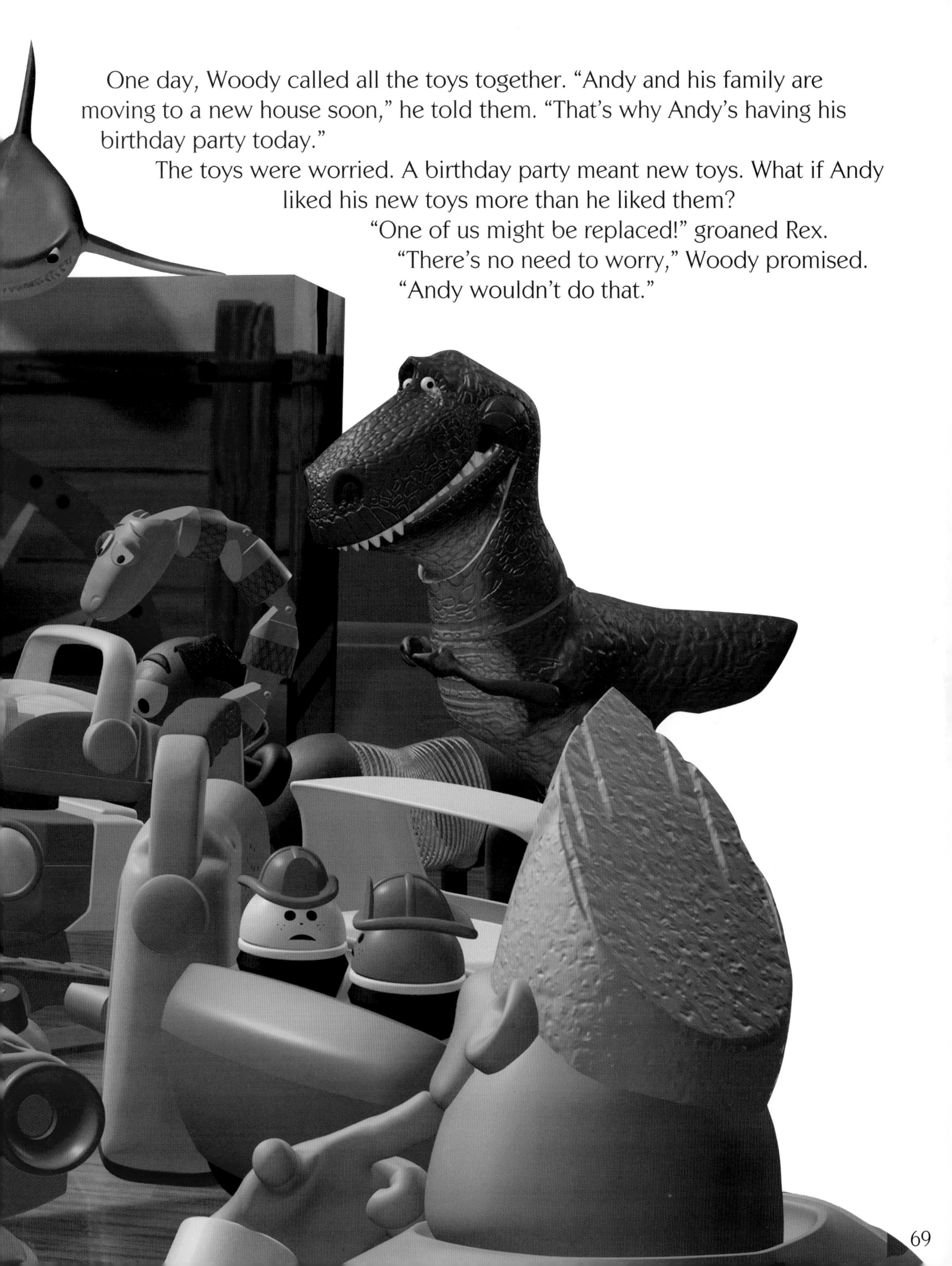

One day, Woody called all the toys together. "Andy and his family are moving to a new house soon," he told them. "That's why Andy's having his birthday party today."

The toys were worried. A birthday party meant new toys. What if Andy liked his new toys more than he liked them?

"One of us might be replaced!" groaned Rex.

"There's no need to worry," Woody promised. "Andy wouldn't do that."

As Andy unwrapped his presents, the toys waited nervously. Everything was all right until the very last parcel – a marvellous spaceman. Andy brought him up to the bedroom and left him there.

"I'm Buzz Lightyear, space ranger," the newcomer said.

Everyone thought Buzz was wonderful. Everyone, that is, except Woody. Woody was jealous!

"You're NOT a space ranger,"he sneered. "You're just a toy like the rest of us!"

Suddenly, they heard barking outside and rushed to the window. Sid, the boy next door, was attacking a toy soldier. His dog, Scud, was watching excitedly.

"Sid's horrible," Rex told Buzz. "He tortures toys just for fun."

The toys watched helplessly as Sid destroyed the soldier.

As the toys went back to their places, Woody was still mad with Buzz. He thought that if he aimed the remote control car at Buzz, the new toy would fall behind the desk and be lost. But the car sped out of control, and everything went wrong – ending up with Buzz falling out of the window. All the toys rushed to the window to see where Buzz had fallen.

"It was an accident!" said Woody. But none of the toys would believe him.

Suddenly, Andy burst into the room. He was going to Pizza Planet and wanted to take a toy.

"I can't find Buzz, Mum," he called. "I'll have to take Woody instead."

But Buzz did go with them! He had fallen into a bush and leapt onto the car just as it drove away.

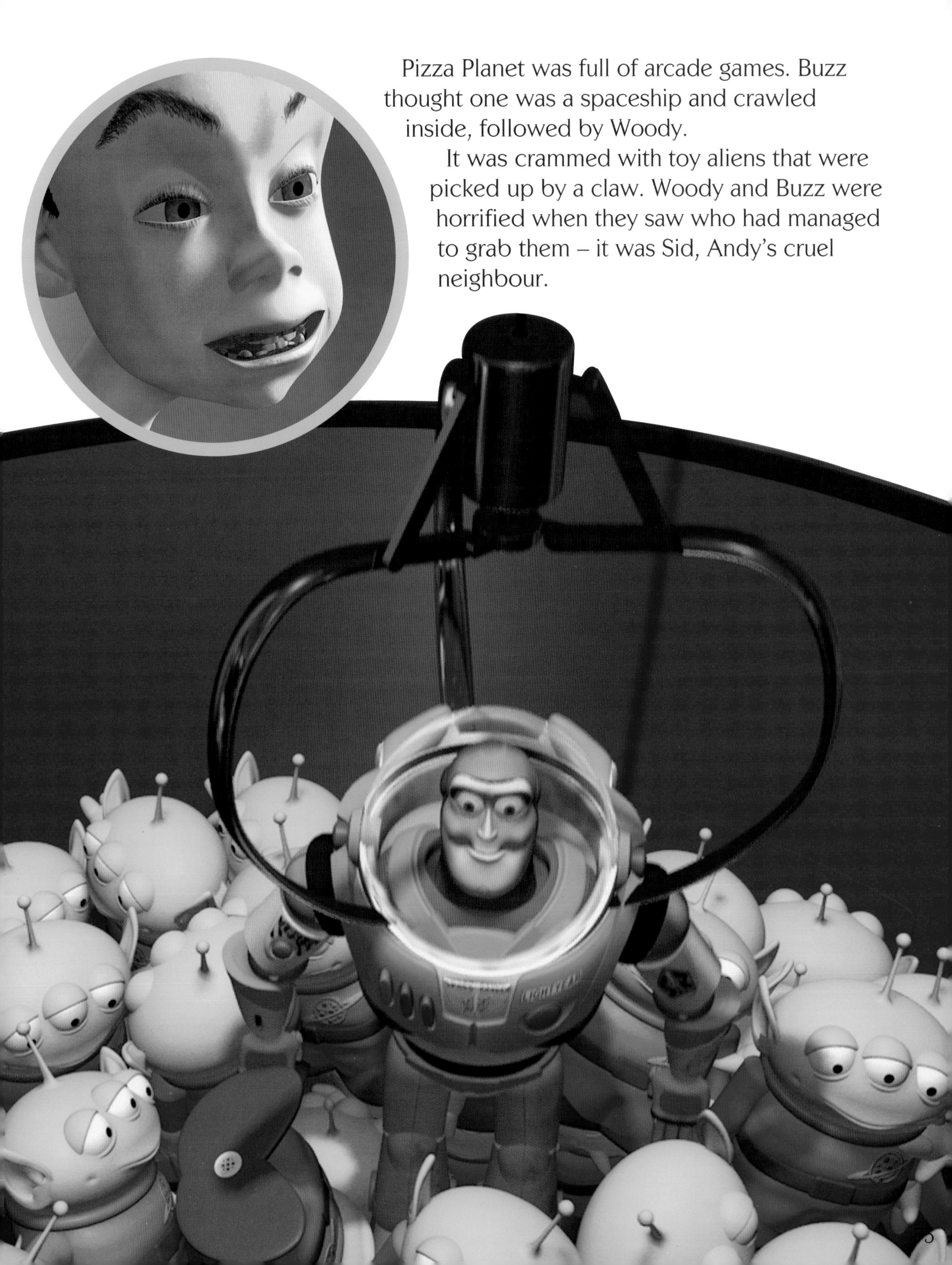

Pizza Planet was full of arcade games. Buzz thought one was a spaceship and crawled inside, followed by Woody.

It was crammed with toy aliens that were picked up by a claw. Woody and Buzz were horrified when they saw who had managed to grab them – it was Sid, Andy's cruel neighbour.

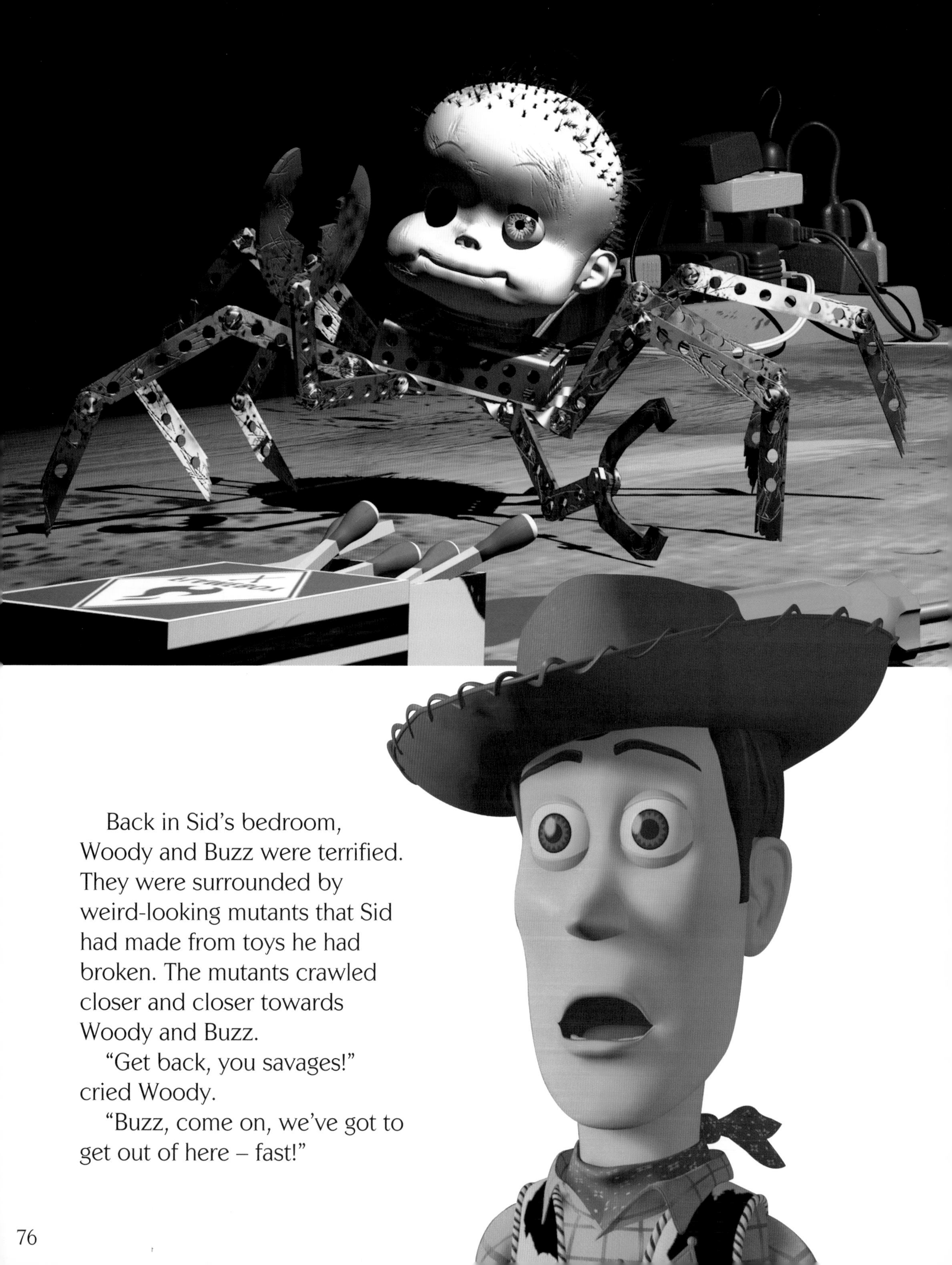

Back in Sid's bedroom, Woody and Buzz were terrified. They were surrounded by weird-looking mutants that Sid had made from toys he had broken. The mutants crawled closer and closer towards Woody and Buzz.

"Get back, you savages!" cried Woody.

"Buzz, come on, we've got to get out of here – fast!"

They had just escaped, when Buzz heard a voice calling:

Buzz left Woody hiding in a cupboard and ran towards the voice. But it was only a television advertisement for the Buzz Lightyear toy. Buzz was stunned. "Is it true?" he whispered. "Am I really… a toy?" Desperate to prove he was a real space ranger, Buzz tried to fly. But he crashed to the floor, breaking his arm.

Woody found Buzz and took him back to Sid's room. Looking out of Sid's window, he saw his old friends in Andy's room.

"Hey guys, help!" Woody called to them, waving madly.

But the toys were angry with Woody because they thought he had hurt Buzz.

Slinky Dog pulled down the blind.

Woody turned sadly away from the window – it seemed that he and Buzz were prisoners in Sid's house.

Luckily, Sid's mutant toys turned out to be friendly after all. That nigh they mended Buzz's arm.

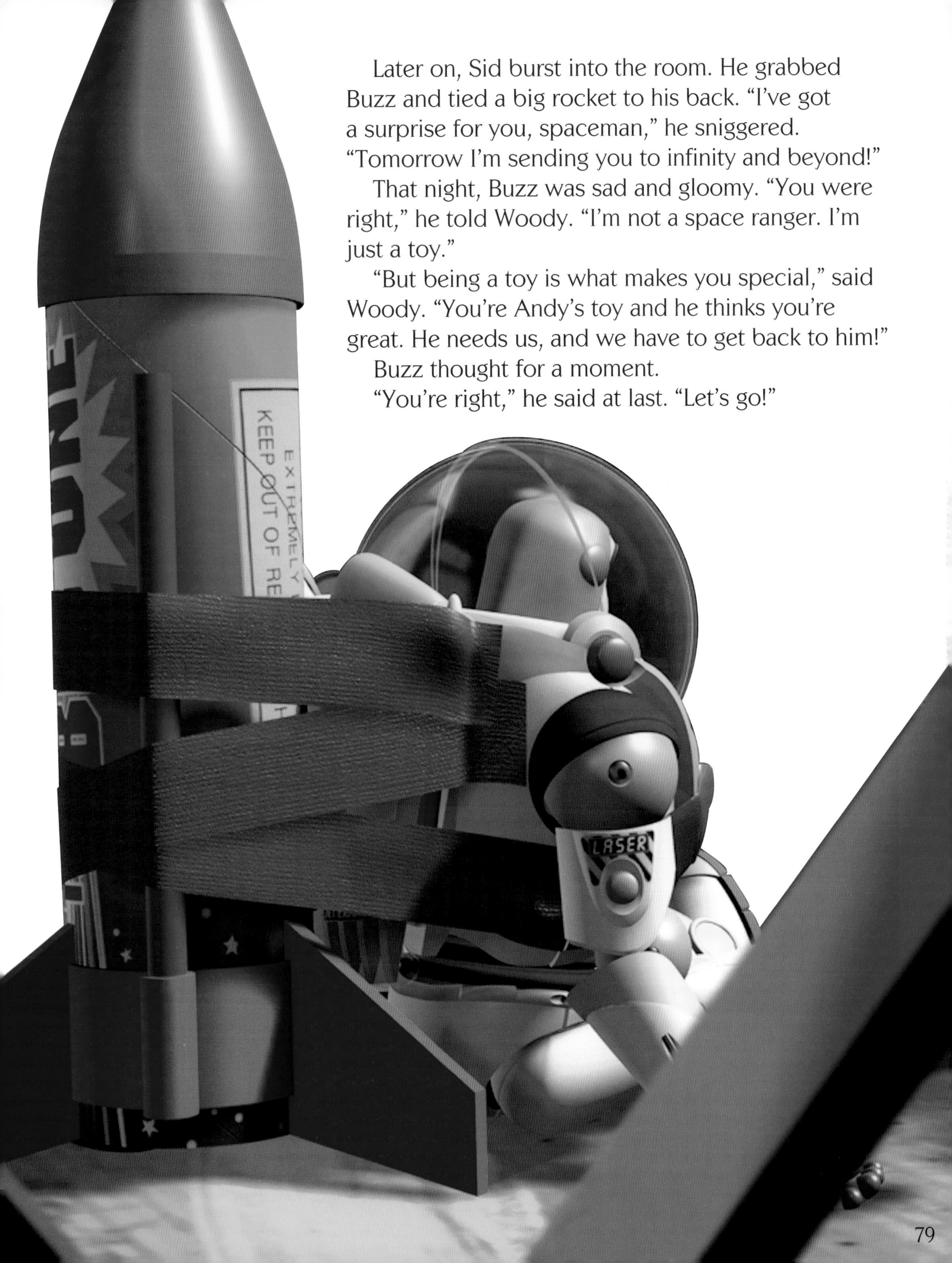


Later on, Sid burst into the room. He grabbed Buzz and tied a big rocket to his back. "I've got a surprise for you, spaceman," he sniggered. "Tomorrow I'm sending you to infinity and beyond!"

That night, Buzz was sad and gloomy. "You were right," he told Woody. "I'm not a space ranger. I'm just a toy."

"But being a toy is what makes you special," said Woody. "You're Andy's toy and he thinks you're great. He needs us, and we have to get back to him!"

Buzz thought for a moment.

"You're right," he said at last. "Let's go!"

But it was too late! **BRRRRRING** rang Sid's alarm clock. Sid reached out, smashed the clock and picked up Buzz.

"Today's the day, spaceman," he said. He rushed downstairs and into the garden, where he started to build a launchpad...

Woody turned to Sid's toys for help.

"Please help me save Buzz," he begged them. "He's my friend." The mutant toys smiled at Woody and nodded. Together, they worked out a plan to rescue Buzz.

Out in the garden, Sid was lighting Buzz's rocket. "Ten! Nine! Eight…" he counted.

10, 9, 8, 7, 6, 5, 4, 3, 2…

Suddenly, Sid spied Woody on the ground. As he picked up the cowboy, his other toys crawled out and surrounded him. Then Woody spoke…

**"AAAAAH!"** yelled Sid.

"Help! These toys are alive!" Screaming, he ran into the house.

Woody and Buzz were free! They thanked the mutant toys for their help and began to make their way home. But Andy's family were just driving away, followed by the removal van!

"It's moving day!" gasped Buzz.

"There they go!" yelled Woody. "Quick! We've got to catch them!"

The two friends rushed after the van. Buzz managed to climb onto the van's back bumper. But Woody was caught by Scud, who had chased them.

"Get away!" shouted Woody, trying to free himself. Scud growled louder...

Bravely, Buzz leapt off the bumper and fought off Scud, who ran back to his house. Now Woody was on the van – but Buzz was stranded on the road!

Woody scrambled into the removal van and found the box that contained Andy's toys. They were amazed to see him!

"Buzz is out there and he's in trouble," Woody told them. "We've got to help him!" He grabbed the remote control car and sent it speeding down the street.

The toys thought Woody was trying to get rid of them, just like he had with Buzz!

Shouting angrily, the toys threw Woody out of the van.

But a moment later, the toys' shouts turned to gasps of amazement as they saw Woody and Buzz come zooming towards them in the remote control car.

"Look! They're together!" said Rex. "Woody was telling the truth, after all."

Then, the car slowed down and stopped.

"The **BATTERIES HAVE RUN DOWN!**" howled Buzz.

Woody and Buzz watched miserably as the van disappeared into the distance.

Suddenly, Buzz remembered something. "Woody! The rocket!" he yelled. Sid's rocket was still tied to his back!

They lit the fuse and **WHOOoSH!** The rocket carried them up into the sky.

Just before it exploded, Buzz pressed a button on his chest. Out popped his wings, freeing them from the rocket.

"We're flying!" laughed Woody, as they soared over the van. Seconds later, they dropped gently through the sunroof of Andy's car.

Woody and Buzz were safe – and they were back with the boy who loved them.

After their adventures, Woody and Buzz became firm friends. Woody no longer felt jealous of Buzz, and the space ranger was happy to be a toy like everyone else. They all settled down together in the new house and the next few months passed happily for everyone.

Christmas came and snow fell thick and soft outside the house. Andy ran downstairs to open his beautifully wrapped Christmas presents.
Once again, the toys watched for the arrival of new toys.

"Nervous, Buzz?" asked Woody.
"No," replied Buzz. "Are you?"
"Tell me, Buzz," laughed Woody. "What could Andy possibly get that would be worse than you?"
The answer came as an excited yelp.
"Oh, no!" laughed the toys –

"A PUPPY!"

THE END

Disney
PRINCESS
Beauty and the Beast

BELLE

THE BEAST

COGSWORTH

STARRING

MRS POTTS
& CHIP

LUMIERE

Disney Princess

# Beauty and the Beast

Once upon a time, a selfish young prince refused to give an old beggar-woman shelter in his castle. But the old woman was really an enchantress. As punishment, she turned the prince into a terrifying beast and cast a spell on everyone in the castle.

Giving the Beast a magic rose she said, "This will bloom until your twenty-first year. If you learn to love another and earn that person's love before the last petal falls, the spell will be broken. If not, you will remain a Beast forever."

In a sleepy village nearby, an eccentric inventor named Maurice lived with his beautiful daughter Belle.

Gaston, a strong and handsome young man from the village, had decided that he wanted to make Belle his wife.

"After all," he told his friend Lefou, "she's the best-looking girl in town. And I deserve the best!"

Gaston arrived at Belle's house, confident that Belle would agree to marry him. But, when he asked her, Belle refused him without a second thought.

She knew she could never marry someone as arrogant and conceited as Gaston!

One day Maurice set off for a fair with his latest invention. As night fell he lost his way and had to seek refuge in the Beast's castle.

Maurice was welcomed by some friendly, enchanted servants, including a candelabra named Lumiere, a clock named Cogsworth, a teapot named Mrs Potts and her son Chip, a teacup.

But the Beast was furious when he discovered a stranger in his home and he threw Maurice into the dungeon. When Maurice's horse returned home alone, Belle set off at once to search for her father.

"Oh, Papa," Belle cried when she found Maurice in the freezing dungeon, "we must get you out of here!"

Sensing danger, Belle turned round. There was the Beast, towering over her and growling loudly.

"Please let my father go," Belle pleaded. "I'll take his place here."

The Beast agreed at once. He dragged Maurice out of the cell and sent him back to the village.

The Beast showed Belle to her room.

"You can go anywhere in the castle," he told her, "except the West Wing. That is forbidden!" Poor Belle was miserable! She missed her father and her home.

The enchanted objects prepared a wonderful meal for her and tried to cheer her up with their singing and dancing.

But Belle was still lonely and later that night she wandered through the castle. She soon found herself in the West Wing. There, among broken furniture and cracked mirrors, she found the magic rose, its petals drooping sadly. Just as Belle reached out to touch the rose, the Beast burst in howling with rage. Terrified, Belle ran out into the snowy night.

Belle leapt on to her father's horse and set off blindly into the dark forest.

Suddenly, she was surrounded by a pack of vicious, hungry wolves.

Just as the wolves closed in for the kill, the Beast appeared through the trees. Fighting bravely, he drove the wolves away.

But then the Beast sank to the ground in pain. The wolves had injured him! Belle knew she could not leave him there alone.

She took the Beast back to the castle and gently tended his bleeding wounds. He seemed quite different now and she was no longer frightened of him.

Meanwhile, at the village tavern, Gaston was still brooding over Belle, even though his friends did their best to cheer him up.

Suddenly, the door burst open and Maurice raced in.

"Help!" he cried. "Belle is being held prisoner by a monstrous Beast!"

The men in the tavern burst out laughing. They thought Maurice was mad! But Gaston smiled to himself. He had thought of a way to make Belle marry him! He called a tall, sinister-looking man over to his table and Gaston began to tell him what he had in mind.

As the days passed, Belle and the Beast spent more and more time together. The enchanted servants were delighted. They were certain that Belle would fall in love with their master and break the spell. But time was running out. Each day more petals fell from the magic rose.

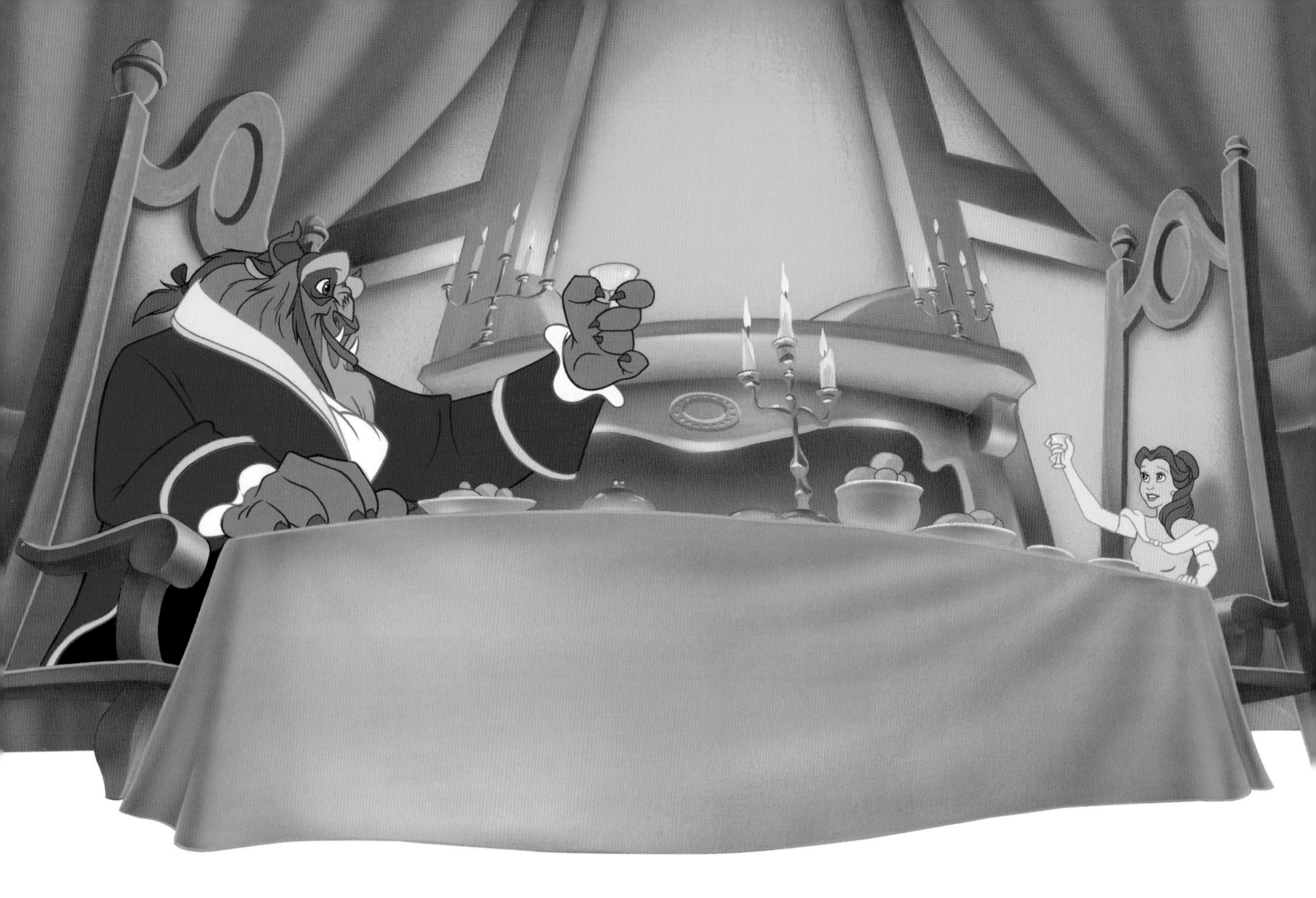

One evening, after dining and dancing together, the Beast and Belle sat out on the terrace in the cool night air.

"Are you happy here, Belle?" asked the Beast.

"Yes," replied Belle. "I just wish I could see my father again."

"You can," said the Beast, and he gave Belle a magic mirror. "This will show you whatever you wish."

"Oh, thank you!" exclaimed Belle. But, as she gazed into it, Belle saw her father lost and trembling with cold as he searched for Belle!

Although the Beast loved Belle, he knew he had to let her go to her father.

"Take the mirror with you," he said sadly, "so you can remember me." Belle set off from the castle and soon found Maurice. She brought him safely home and put him to bed.

The next day Gaston arrived at Belle's house with a crowd of villagers. He said that Maurice would be taken to an asylum unless Belle agreed to marry him.

"My father's not mad!" cried Belle.

"He must be," said Lefou. "He was raving about a monstrous beast!"

"The Beast is real!" cried Belle. "Look!"

She held up the magic mirror and the crowd saw the Beast for themselves. They all shouted with fear and refused to listen to Belle when she told them the Beast was kind and good.

Furious that his plan had failed, Gaston gathered the mob together to attack the Beast's castle.

The men marched up to the castle doors and broke them down. Cogsworth led the enchanted servants in a brave defence of the castle. But the Beast missed Belle and was too heartbroken to fight, even when Gaston beat him with a club and drove him on to the castle roof.

Only when he heard Belle's voice did the Beast look up.

"You came back!" he cried, rushing to embrace Belle.

This was the chance Gaston had been waiting for.

Drawing his dagger, he stabbed the Beast in the back. But as the Beast collapsed, Gaston tripped – and fell tumbling from the roof.

Belle ran to the wounded Beast and bent to kiss him. The last petal was just about to fall from the rose.

"You can't die," sobbed Belle. "I love you! I wish I had never left you alone!"

Suddenly, a magic mist surrounded the Beast and, before Belle's astonished eyes, he changed into the handsome young prince he had once been.

One by one, the enchanted servants became human again. Weeping with joy, they hugged each other as the Prince swept Belle into his arms.

The Prince had found his true love at last and the spell of the enchantress was broken. As the sun burst through the clouds, they knew they would all live together in happiness for ever after.

THE END

Disney · PIXAR
RATATOUILLE
(rat•a•too•ee)

REMY
EMILE
STARRING
COLETTE
LINGUINI
SKINNER

Disney · PIXAR
RATATOUILLE
(rat·a·too·ee)

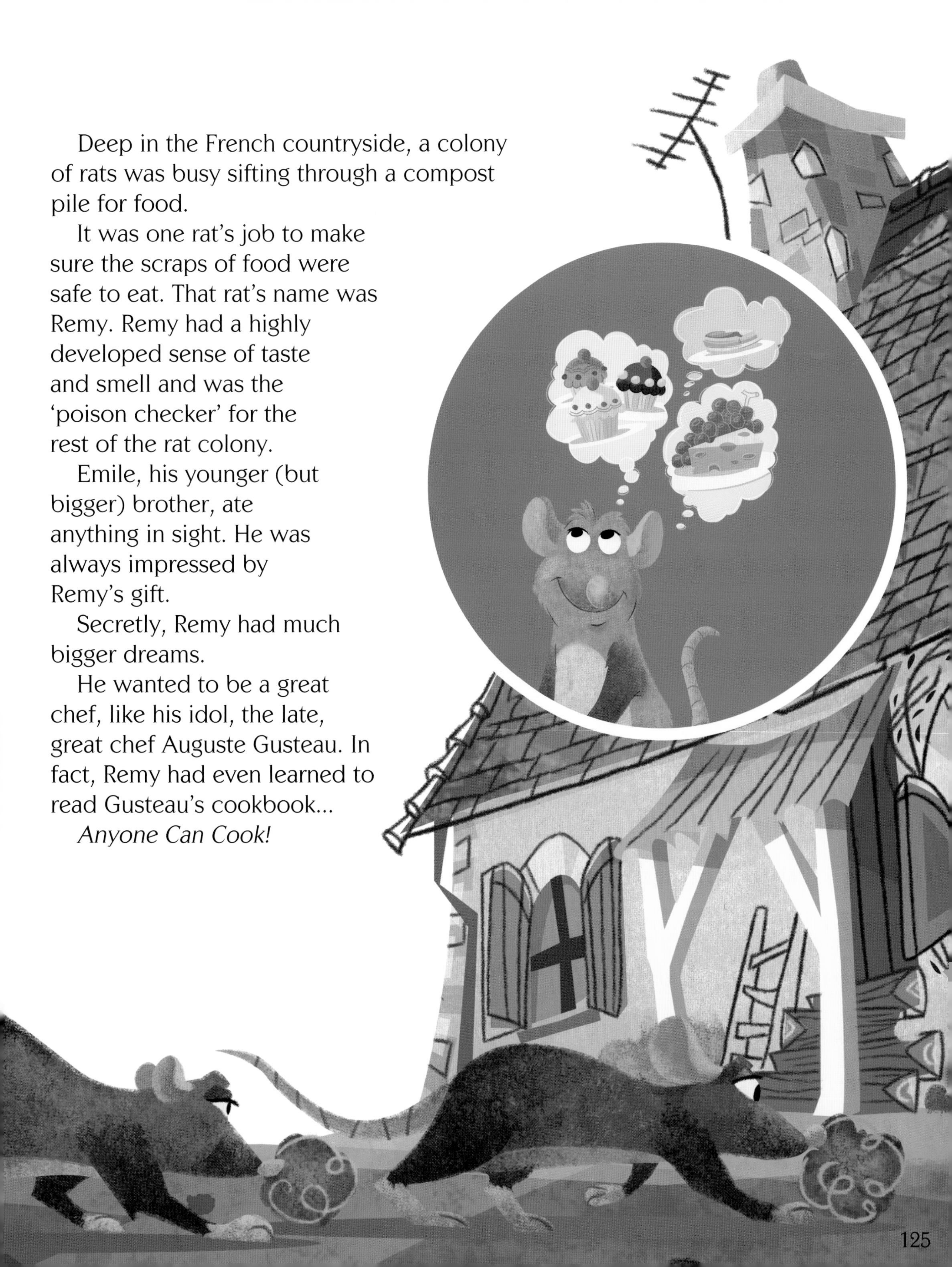

Deep in the French countryside, a colony of rats was busy sifting through a compost pile for food.

It was one rat's job to make sure the scraps of food were safe to eat. That rat's name was Remy. Remy had a highly developed sense of taste and smell and was the 'poison checker' for the rest of the rat colony.

Emile, his younger (but bigger) brother, ate anything in sight. He was always impressed by Remy's gift.

Secretly, Remy had much bigger dreams.

He wanted to be a great chef, like his idol, the late, great chef Auguste Gusteau. In fact, Remy had even learned to read Gusteau's cookbook...

*Anyone Can Cook!*

Both the cookbook and the compost pile belonged to an old woman named Mabel. Her attic was home to the entire rat colony, though she didn't know it.

One day, Remy and Emile sneaked into her kitchen together. Remy always enjoyed looking for spices in her cupboards.

The nervous Emile did not. Their father, Django, always said humans were dangerous and to stay far away from them.

Suddenly, Remy raced from the kitchen to the TV. He saw his idol Gusteau! Remy learned that Gusteau had died from a broken heart when his restaurant lost its five-star status.

Remy was so shocked by the news about Gusteau that he didn't notice Mabel waking up.

He and Emile had to scramble to escape as Mabel chased them. In the chaos, the ceiling cracked and the entire rat colony fell to the floor.

"Evacuate!" Django shouted to the rats.

As the other rats headed out the door, Remy went back into the kitchen for the cookbook. He couldn't leave it behind.

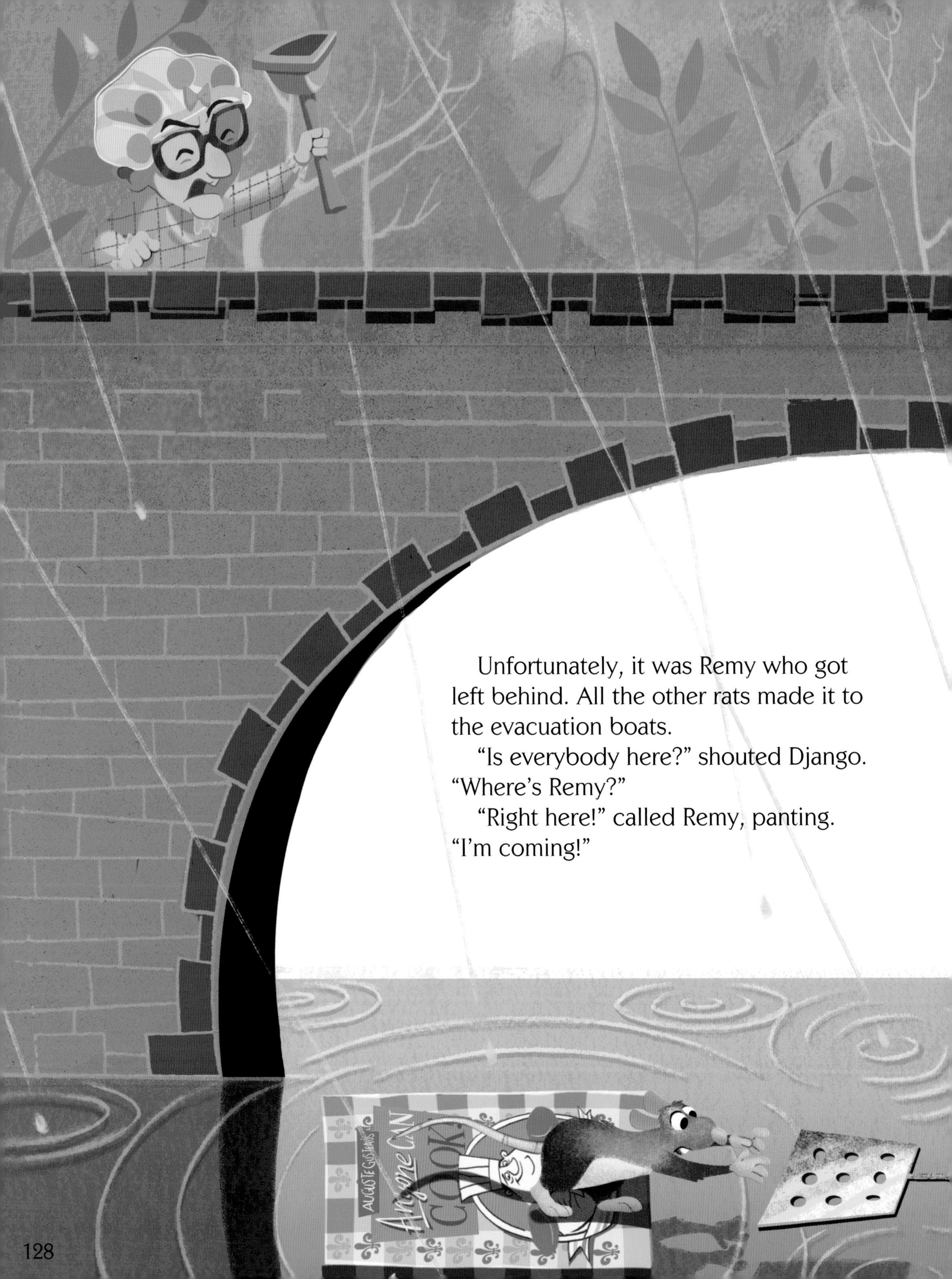


Unfortunately, it was Remy who got left behind. All the other rats made it to the evacuation boats.

"Is everybody here?" shouted Django. "Where's Remy?"

"Right here!" called Remy, panting. "I'm coming!"

Remy threw the cookbook into the water and hopped on board.

"Come on, son!" called Django. "You can make it!"

Poor Remy didn't make it. Separated from his family, the little rat swept down the sewer currents. Hungry, sad and wet, he finally found a landing place, and started drying out the pages of his cookbook. Suddenly, Gusteau seemed to come to life on a page in the cookbook. "If you are hungry, go up and look around," said Gusteau. "If you focus on what you've left behind, you will never be able to see what lies ahead."

So Remy climbed up and up until he saw…

"Paris?" he said breathlessly, taking in the view. "All this time I've been underneath Paris? Wow! It's beautiful!"

"The most beautiful," said Gusteau with a sigh.

Remy looked to his left. His jaw dropped. The sign for Gusteau's restaurant was right nearby.

"Your restaurant?" Remy said to Gusteau. "You've led me to your restaurant!"

To Remy, this was a dream come true.

Remy had made his way to a skylight in the roof of the restaurant. Gusteau appeared again and they looked down at the kitchen. Right at that moment, an awkward young man named Linguini arrived with a letter for Skinner, the ill-tempered chef in charge of the kitchen. Linguini's mother, who recently died, had been a good friend of Gusteau's, and Linguini was hoping to get a job at the restaurant.

"We've already hired him," said Larousse, one of the chefs.

Skinner had no choice. The ungainly Linguini would work in the kitchen as a garbage boy.

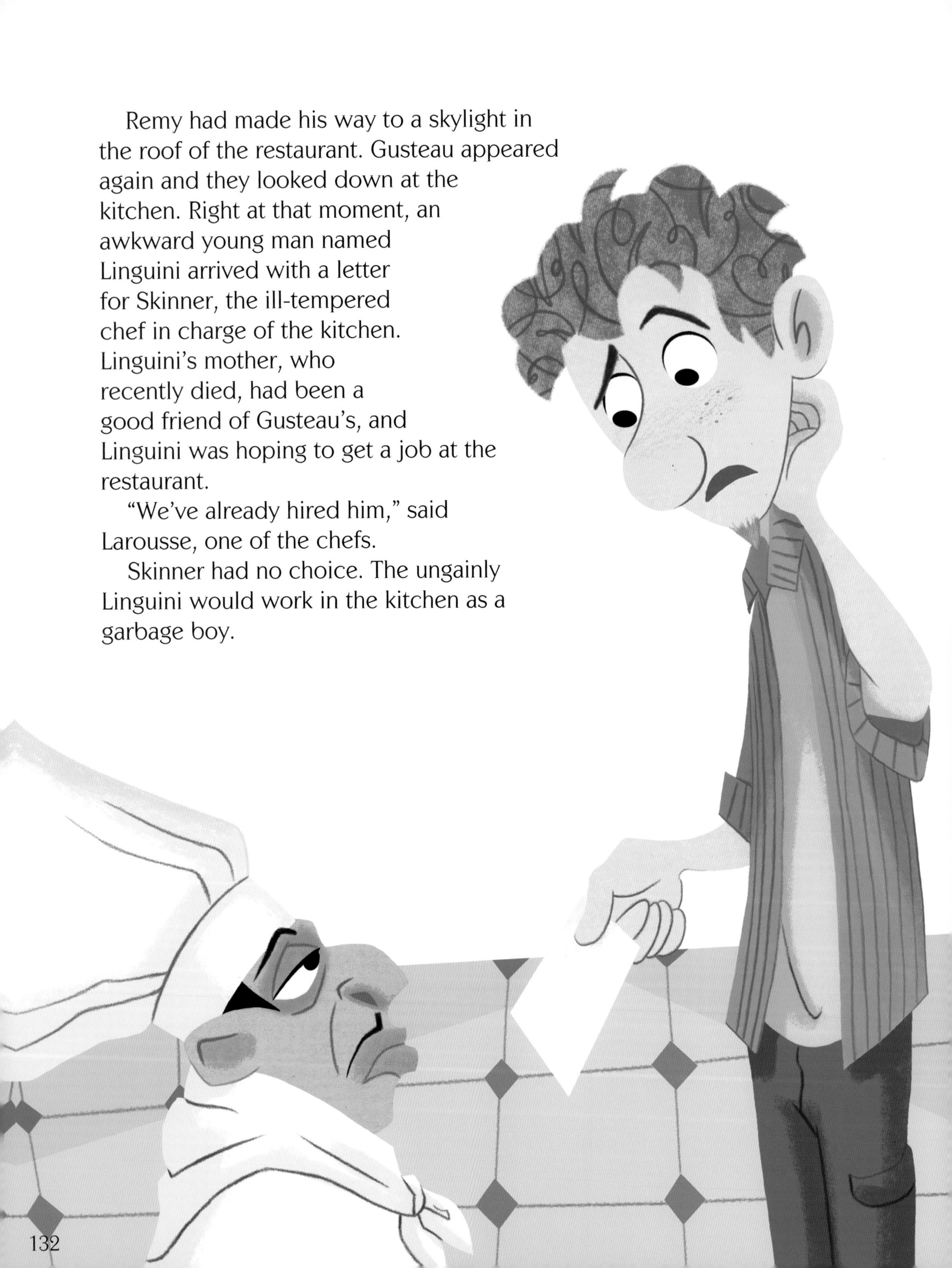

Linguini went right to work, but he was very clumsy. Remy watched in horror from the skylight as Linguini accidentally spilled a pot of soup and secretly began adding ingredients to try and fix it.

"Do something!" Remy shouted to the figure of Gusteau.

"He's ruining the soup!"

Gusteau shrugged. "What can I do? I'm a figment of your imagination."

Then, suddenly, the skylight fell open, and Remy tumbled downwards, landing in the kitchen! Quickly, he scrambled across the kitchen floor, careful to not be seen by any humans. Remy was determined to escape through an open window.

Then he smelled Linguini's horrible soup - and stopped short. This was Remy's chance. He could fix the soup! He jumped to the stovetop and started carefully choosing ingredients to put into the pot.

Suddenly, Linguini was staring right at Remy and Skinner was right behind them! Linguini quickly hid Remy under a colander.

"How dare you cook in my kitchen!" shouted Skinner, who had spotted Linguini holding a ladle. He fired Linguini on the spot.

But worse things were happening. While Skinner was yelling the waiter whisked a bowl of the soup off to the dining room to an important food critic.

As the chefs waited nervously in the kitchen, word came back from the waiter. The soup was delicious! The critic loved it!

Colette, one of the cooks, looked at Linguini. "You can't fire him!" she said to Skinner. "Wasn't Gusteau's motto that anyone can cook? Linguini should be given a chance to cook in the kitchen. Besides, how would it look if the restaurant fired the person who created the soup that a critic liked?"

Angrily, Skinner gave in, and assigned Colette to teach Linguini in the kitchen.

In the commotion, Remy made a move for the window. But Skinner spotted him. He made Linguini catch the rat in a jar.

"Take it away from here, far way. Dispose of it. Go!"

Poor Linguini didn't have the heart to throw Remy in the river. He started talking to him instead. When Remy nodded, Linguini realized Remy understood what he was saying!

"Wait. You can cook, right?" asked Linguini. Linguini made a deal with Remy. Linguini would let Remy out if Remy promised to help him cook. But as soon as Linguini opened the jar, Remy ran away. Then Remy stopped and turned back. This could be his big chance to cook in a real gourmet kitchen! The little rat decided to give the partnership a try.

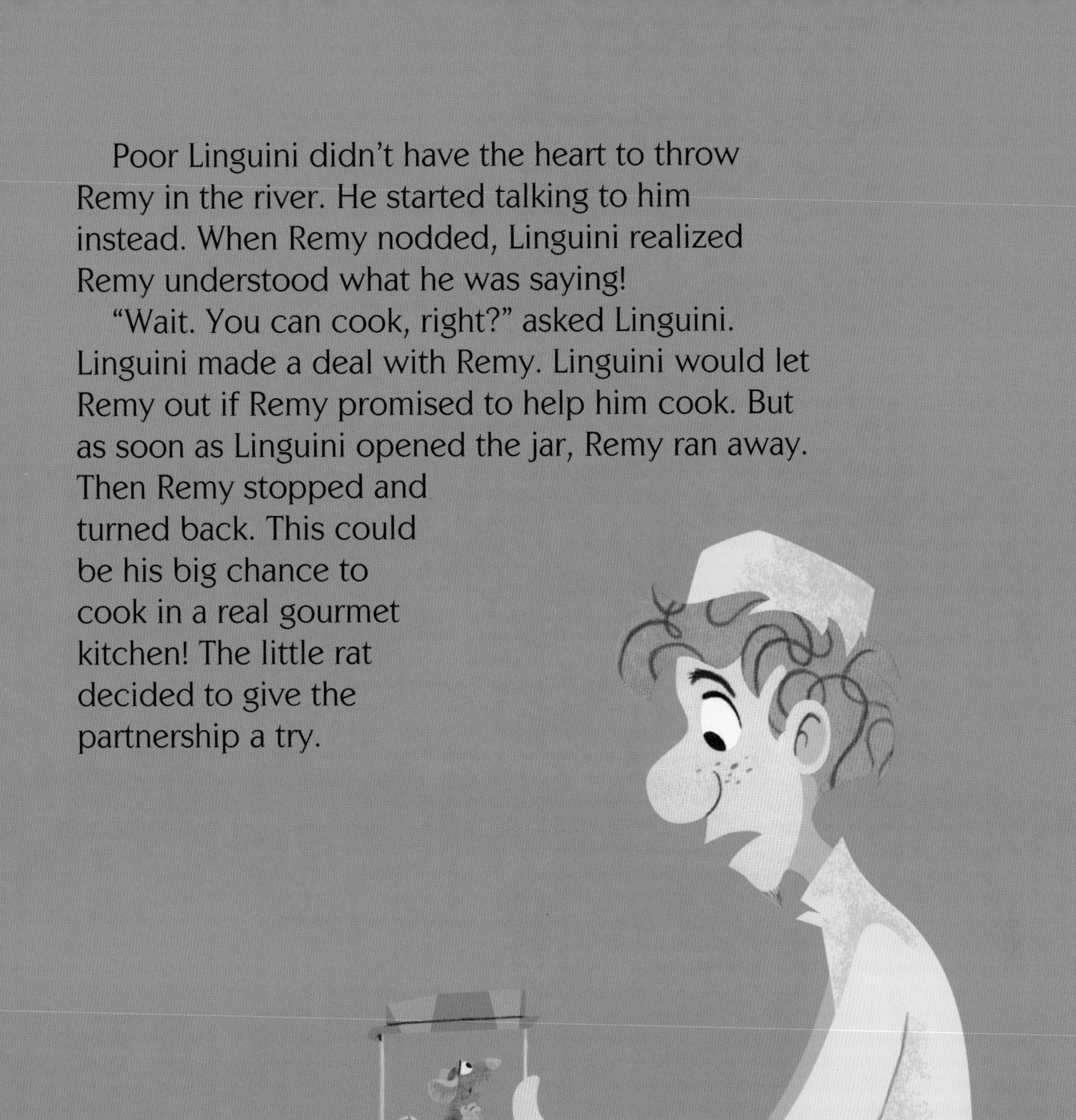

Back in the kitchen, Linguini hid Remy in his shirt and Remy tried to help Linguini with his cooking. Remy tried to guide Linguini by biting and tickling him, but it wasn't working.

Suddenly, Skinner burst through the door and caught a glimpse of Remy. "The rat! I saw it!" shouted the nasty little man.

Linguini quickly hid Remy in his hat and ducked out – almost colliding with a waiter! But Remy tugged Linguini's hair at the last minute and Linguini jerked backwards like a puppet. Could this be their new system?

Linguini and Remy went home to practise cooking. Remy guided Linguini by tugging his hair and before too long, Linguini could even cook blindfolded!

In the meantime, Skinner finally read the letter from Linguini's mother and was now keeping a secret: Auguste Gusteau was Linguini's father. Nobody knew, not even Linguini…or Gusteau!

That meant the restaurant rightfully belonged to Linguini. Skinner was horrified. He had always thought the restaurant would be his! He had to do something to make sure Linguini never found out.

One night, Remy was relaxing in the alley behind the restaurant, enjoying his cooking success, when Emile appeared.

Emile led his long-lost brother to the rat colony's new home. There, in honour of Remy's homecoming, a hopping party filled the sewer with music and dancing.

But soon, Remy said he had to leave. He tried to explain that he had new friends, a job, even a new place to live. In fact…he was living with a human. Django scowled and tried to convince his son that humans were dangerous. But Remy was sure that his situation was different, that Linguini was different. Against his father's wishes, Remy headed back to the restaurant.

Not long afterwards, Remy found the papers in Skinner's office saying that Linguini was the rightful owner of the restaurant.

Suddenly, Skinner appeared! Remy grabbed both the will and the letter, and ran. Skinner chased him. Skinner did not want those papers to get into the wrong hands! Remy held the papers in his mouth, using them almost like wings, to glide onto a boat. The chef ended up in the river.

By the time the soaking-wet Skinner got back to Gusteau's, Linguini was in his office with Colette. Linguini knew the truth now, and he fired Skinner on the spot.

Over the next few weeks, the restaurant became more and more popular. But Linguini stopped paying attention to cooking, and Remy didn't like it. Neither did Colette. Linguini even held a press conference in the dining room of the restaurant. He was enjoying the attention a bit too much.

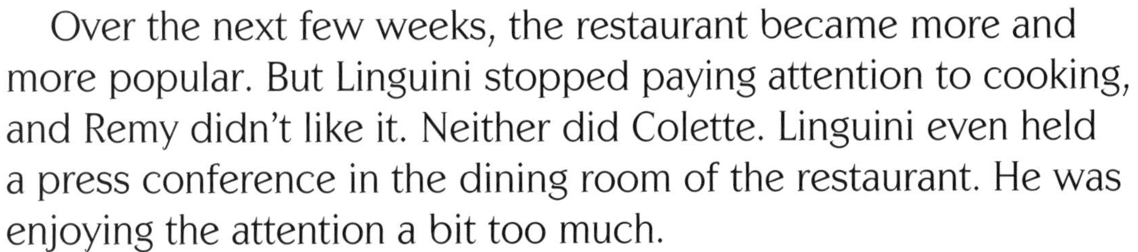

Suddenly, the famous critic Ego – the very same Ego who had ruined Gusteau's – arrived and gave his warning: "I will return tomorrow night with high expectations."

After Ego's announcement, Colette dragged Linguini back to the kitchen, with Remy in tow. Remy was furious that Linguini wasn't more worried about cooking, and he yanked Linguini's hair, hard.

Linguini got angry. He took Remy out to the back and said, "You take a break, Little Chef. I'm not your puppet."

Remy was cross with Linguini. Later that night, Remy showed the entire rat colony how to get into the walk-in refrigerator and told them to take whatever they wanted.

That's when Linguini returned to apologize.

"You're stealing from me?" Linguini furiously asked Remy. "I thought you were my friend. I trusted you! Get out and don't ever come back!"

But Remy did come back. He felt horrible. Plus, Ego had come to review the restaurant. Remy knew his friend Linguini needed help. Boldly, Remy walked alone through the doors, into the bustling kitchen.

"Rat!" shrieked all the chefs.

"Don't touch him!" shouted Linguini. "The truth is, I have no talent at all. But this rat – he's the cook."

From the shadows, Django watched the human defend Remy!

Still, the cooks walked out – even Colette.

Only Remy and Linguini were left to cook for Anton Ego.

"I was wrong about you. About him," Django told Remy, referring to how Linguini stood up for the little rat. "I'm proud of you."

Django whistled, and rats instantly filled the kitchen. "We're not cooks, but you tell us what to do and we'll get it done."

When the health inspector arrived, Django sent a team of rats to whisk him away. After going through the dishwasher to clean themselves, the other rats began to cook.

Even Colette came back. She was a little shocked to see all the rats, but she soon agreed to help cook the dish Remy had chosen for Ego. It was ratatouille.

Linguini, acting as waiter, served the dish to Ego. The delicious ratatouille brought back a warm, comforting memory from Ego's childhood. When Ego asked to meet the chef, Linguini and Colette waited until all the other customers left the restaurant, then they brought out Remy.

The next morning Ego gave the restaurant a rave review!

Unfortunately, the health inspector closed down Gusteau's, but not all was lost for Remy and his friends. Ego retired and invested in a small but quaint bistro, La Ratatouille. Linguine was the waiter, and Colette cooked - along with one very special, little chef. The restaurant would become well loved by its customers, both big and small.

Remy's dreams had finally come true.

THE END

Disney • PIXAR

# WALL•E

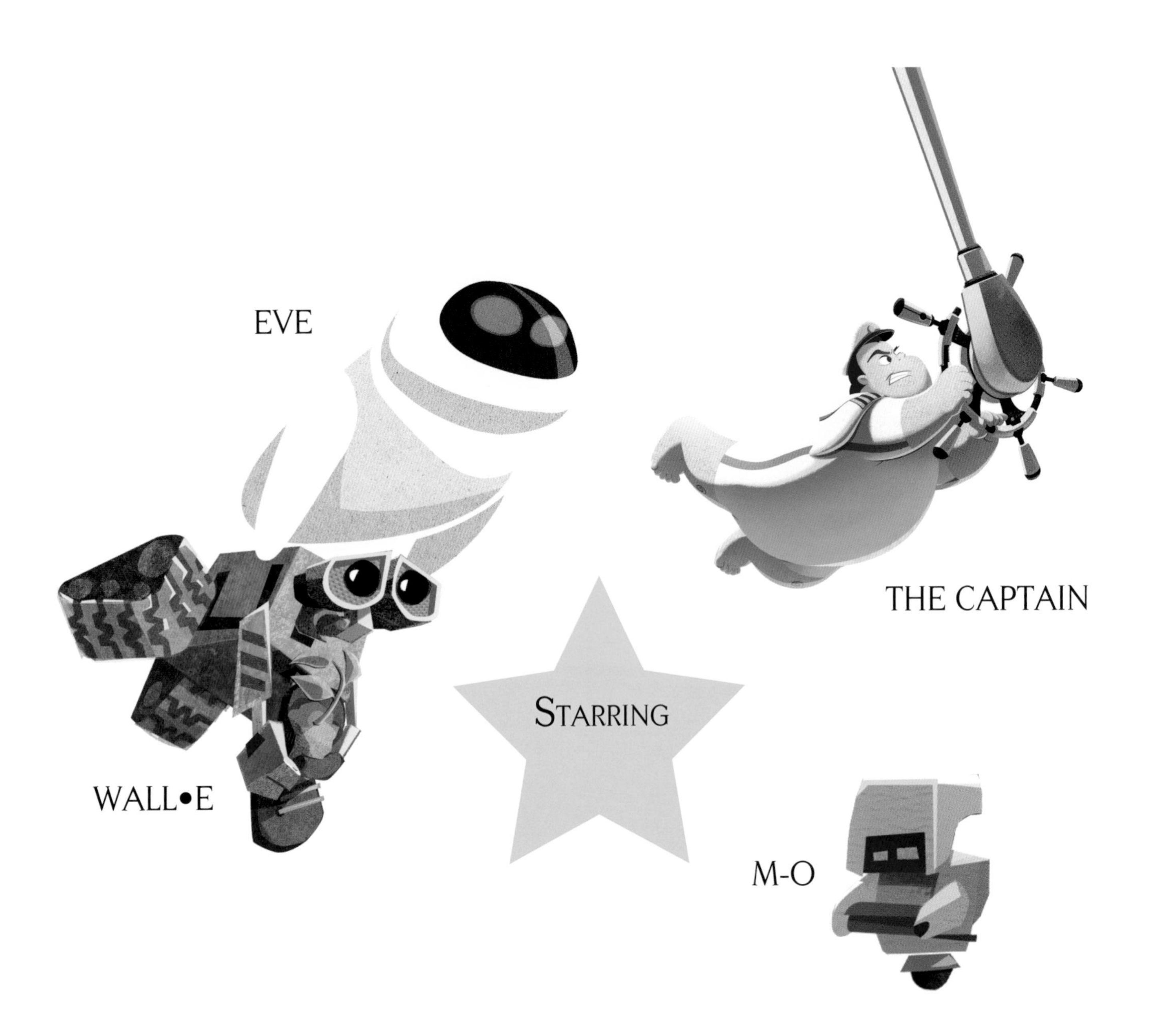
EVE
THE CAPTAIN
STARRING
WALL•E
M-O

Disney • PIXAR

# WALL•E

If you lived back in the 29th century, you would live off in space with all the other people from Earth.

Long ago, Earth had been evacuated because it was too polluted. No one could live there until someone cleaned up the planet. And there was someone – just one – left behind to do that work.

WALL•E was a Waste Allocation Load Lifter, Earth-Class. He didn't mind his lonely job of compacting trash. He looked at it as a sort of treasure hunt. He never knew what he would find each day in the trash.

BnL

But WALL•E wanted more in life. He didn't ask for much. He just wanted to hold hands with someone – someone he loved. He had seen this watching his favourite movie over and over. It was his dream.

One day, WALL•E was out compacting and cubing trash when he found something special. It was a plant. His pet cockroach chirped, knowing that his friend would be really interested in this green thing. Neither one of them had ever seen anything like it before. WALL•E took it home.

Soon afterwards, another robot landed on Earth. WALL•E fell in love with the sleek new robot at first sight. Her name was EVE, and over time, WALL•E figured out that she was looking for something. But she wouldn't tell him what it was.

WALL•E took her to his home and showed her all the treasures he had collected from the trash.

But when WALL•E showed her the plant, she grabbed it from him and stored it in a secret compartment in her chest.

Then she shut down. She slept and slept, no matter how hard WALL•E tried to wake her up.

Soon EVE's ship returned to take her away. No! WALL•E loved her. He didn't want her to leave. So he latched onto the outside of her ship and followed her into space.

The spaceship docked inside an enormous ship called the *Axiom*. The Captain's robot assistant, Gopher, wrapped EVE in energy bands and drove her away. WALL•E raced after her. And M-O, a cleaner-bot, chased WALL•E. (M-O was programmed to clean, clean, clean. WALL•E, the little trash-compacting robot from Earth, was his biggest challenge ever.)

As WALL•E chased EVE, he accidentally disabled passenger Mary's electronic system. Mary blinked and looked around.

She saw the world around her, instead of viewing it all digitally over her holo-screen. She liked the change.

Finally EVE was ready to give the plant to the Captain. By doing so, she would prove that Earth was clean enough that a plant could now grow there. That meant everyone could return to the planet.

But EVE's compartment was empty. The plant had disappeared!

Disappointed, the Captain sent EVE to the repair ward, along with WALL•E. When they got there, WALL•E thought some orderlies were hurting EVE. So he helped her escape, along with all the reject-bots from the repair ward.

But there was a problem. Once they ran free, they looked like escaped convicts. A warning broadcast their escape throughout the *Axiom*. The ship's stewards tried to catch them.

To avoid being captured, EVE took WALL•E to an escape pod. She would send him to Earth where he would be safe, and then she could find the plant. Instead, Gopher appeared. He had the plant! He put it in the escape pod. WALL•E and the plant were launched into space – not towards Earth, but far into outer space! WALL•E panicked and pushed a lot of buttons.

WALL•E pushed the wrong button. The pod exploded, but he escaped. EVE went to try to help him. Whoosh! WALL•E zoomed up to EVE . . . and showed her that he had saved the plant. Delighted, she leaned in towards him, and an arc of electricity passed between their foreheads – a robot kiss.

Soon they were floating
in space, dancing and giggling.

Back on the *Axiom*, WALL•E tried to wait as EVE delivered the plant to the Captain. The Captain was so excited that he was ready to return to Earth, but Auto wouldn't let him.

Quickly Gopher snatched the plant and dumped it down the trash chute. It hit WALL•E. The little bot was climbing up to get to EVE. Happily he delivered the plant right to her. But Auto electrocuted WALL•E and sent him back down the chute with EVE.

WALL•E and EVE ended up in the ship's garbage bay. EVE rescued the injured little bot while WALL•E tried to give her the plant. He still thought she wanted it more than anything else. But WALL•E was wrong. EVE just wanted to help WALL•E now. M-O helped, still trying to clean WALL•E.

Soon EVE flew all three of them up and out of the garbage bay, with the plant in hand. She wanted to get WALL•E home to Earth so she could find the right parts to fix him.

The Captain was fighting Auto for control of the ship by now. He sent a message to EVE, telling her to take the plant to a large machine called the holo-detector. It would scan the plant and ready the ship to head towards Earth. That was all EVE cared about now.

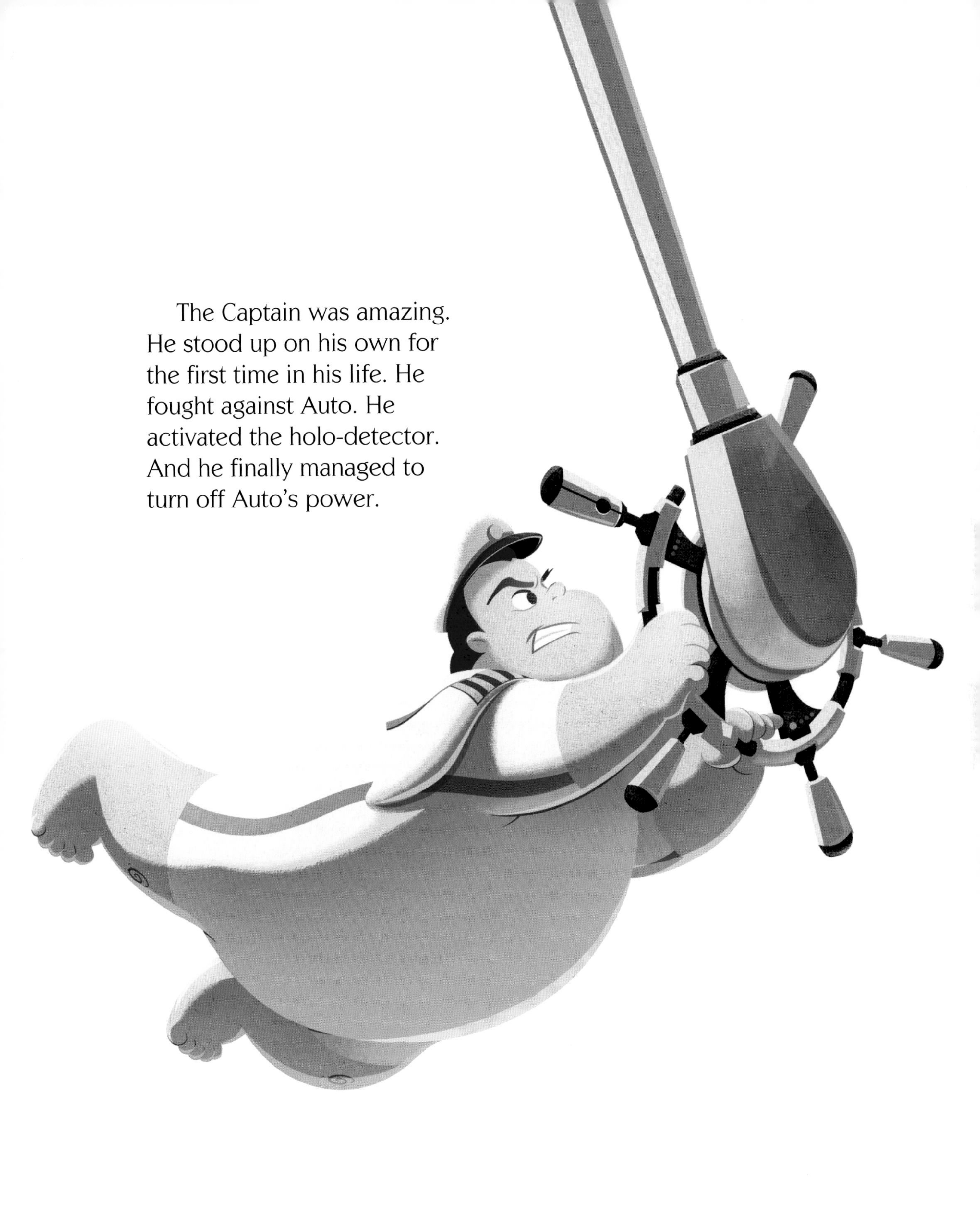

The Captain was amazing. He stood up on his own for the first time in his life. He fought against Auto. He activated the holo-detector. And he finally managed to turn off Auto's power.

EVE fought to reach the holo-detector. At last she put the plant inside the machine. The holo-detector scanned the plant. Finally they could return to Earth.

But not all was well. WALL•E had been crushed by the giant machine, trying to keep it up high enough.

Heartbroken, EVE pulled WALL•E's crushed body from under the holo-detector.

More determined than before, EVE wanted to take him home to his truck where she could find the right parts to bring him back to life.

As soon as the *Axiom* landed on Earth, EVE headed straight for WALL•E's home and began to repair him. At last, he powered up . . . and began cubing trash. Something was wrong. He was just another trash-cubing robot. All the love was gone. He didn't even recognize EVE.

Sadly, EVE held WALL•E's hand and leaned towards him.

An electric arc passed between their heads – the robot kiss. She was saying good-bye.

Then . . . WALL•E's hand began to move. EVE looked into his eyes. He was coming back to life! He recognized her!

"Ee-vah?" he said.

After following EVE across the universe, WALL•E had ended up right where he had started: home. But this time, he had the one thing he had always wanted – EVE's hand clasped in his own.

THE END

Disney
THE
LION KING

PUMBAA
SIMBA
SCAR
TIMON
STARRING
MUFASA
NALA
ZAZU
RAFIKI

# THE LION KING

As the morning sun rose high over the African plain, animals and birds gathered at the foot of Pride Rock.

"There he is!" one of them cried suddenly. "There's the new Prince!" Everyone cheered and stamped their feet. "Welcome Prince Simba!" they shouted.

They watched in silence as Rafiki, a wise old baboon, raised the lion cub high in the air. The clouds parted and the sun's rays shone down on the future King. Slowly Rafiki lowered his arms and took Simba back to his proud parents, King Mufasa and Queen Sarabi.

It was a very special day.

Time passed quickly for little Simba. There was so much to learn. One morning the King showed his son round the kingdom. “Remember,” Mufasa warned, “a good king must respect all creatures, for we exist together in the great Circle of Life.”

Later that day Simba met his uncle, Scar. The cub proudly told him that he had seen the whole of his future kingdom.

"Even beyond the northern border?" Scar asked slyly.

"Well, no," said Simba sadly. "My father has forbidden me to go there."

"Quite right," said Scar. "Only the bravest lions go there. An elephant graveyard is no place for a young prince."

Simba hurried away to find his best friend, a young lioness called Nala. Even though he knew it was wrong, Simba had decided to visit the elephant graveyard with Nala that very day.

He had no idea that Scar had ordered three hyenas to go to the elephant graveyard too. Scar wanted them to kill the cub as the first step in his plan to take over Mufasa's kingdom.

Simba raced ahead across the plains, leading Nala to the forbidden place. Eventually they reached a pile of bones and Simba knew they had arrived.

"It's creepy here." said Nala. "Where are we?"

“This is the elephant graveyard!” Simba cried. He was looking at a skull when he saw Zazu, his father’s adviser.

“You must leave here immediately!” Zazu commanded. “You are in great danger.”

But it was already too late! They were trapped. Three hyenas had surrounded them, laughing menacingly.

Simba took a deep breath and tried to roar – but only a squeaky rumble came out. The hyenas laughed hysterically.

Simba took another deep breath.

ROAARR! The three hyenas looked round into the eyes of – King Mufasa.

The hyenas fled howling into the mist.

Mufasa sent Nala and Zazu ahead and walked slowly home with his son. "Simba, I'm disappointed in you. You disobeyed me and put yourself and others in great danger."

Simba felt terrible. "I was only trying to be brave like you," he tried to explain.

"Being brave doesn't mean you go looking for trouble," said the King gently.

The moon shone brightly above them and the stars twinkled in the dark sky.
Mufasa stopped. “Look at the stars! From there the great kings of the past look down on us. Just remember that they’ll always be there to guide you, and so will I.”
Simba nodded. “I’ll remember.”

By the next day Scar had devised another plan to get rid of Mufasa and Simba. He led Simba to the bottom of a gorge and told him to wait for his father. Then the hyenas started a stampede among a herd of wildebeest.

At that moment Mufasa was walking along a ridge with Zazu. "Simba!" he cried. "I'm coming!"

The King raced down the gorge and rescued his son, but he could not save himself.

He fell onto an overhanging rock as the wildebeest swept by him. Looking up he saw his brother.

"Scar, help me!" he cried. But Scar just leaned over and whispered, "Long live the King!" Then he pushed Mufasa into the path of the trampling wildebeest.

When the stampede was over, Simba ran to his father's side.

"Father," he whimpered, nuzzling Mufasa's mane. But the King did not reply, and Simba started sobbing.

"Simba," said Scar coldly, "what have you done? This is all your fault," he lied. "The King is dead and you must never show your face in the pride again. Run away and never return."

As Scar returned to take the royal throne at Pride Rock for himself, Simba stumbled exhausted and frightened through the grasslands towards the jungle. He took a few more shaky steps and collapsed. Hungry vultures circled above him.

Eventually Simba opened his eyes. A warthog, called Pumbaa, and Timon, a meerkat, were gazing down at him. They poured water into his dry mouth.

"You nearly died," said Pumbaa. "We saved you."

"Thanks for your help," said Simba, "but it doesn't matter. I've nowhere to go."

"Why not stay with us?" said Timon, kindly. "Put your past behind you. Remember! Hakuna matata – no worries! That's the way we live."

Simba thought for a moment and decided to stay in the jungle with his new friends.

Many years later, deep in a cave, Rafiki stared at a picture of a lion. "It is time," he said, smiling, and prepared to leave.

The very next day Simba rescued Pumbaa from a hungry lioness – it was Nala! The two friends were delighted to see each other again. Nala told Simba about Scar's reign of terror at Pride Rock and begged him to return. "With you alive, Scar has no right to the throne," she said.

"I can't go back. I'm not fit to be a king," Simba said sadly.

"You could be," Nala told him.

Simba showed Nala his favourite places in the jungle. “It’s beautiful,” she said. “I can see why you like it – but it’s not your home. You’re hiding from the future.” She turned and left her friend alone.

That night Simba lay by a stream thinking. He heard a noise and looked up.

"Come with me," said Rafiki.

"I will take you to your father."

Simba followed him in wonder to the edge of the stream. As Simba looked into the water, his reflection gradually changed shape and became his father's!

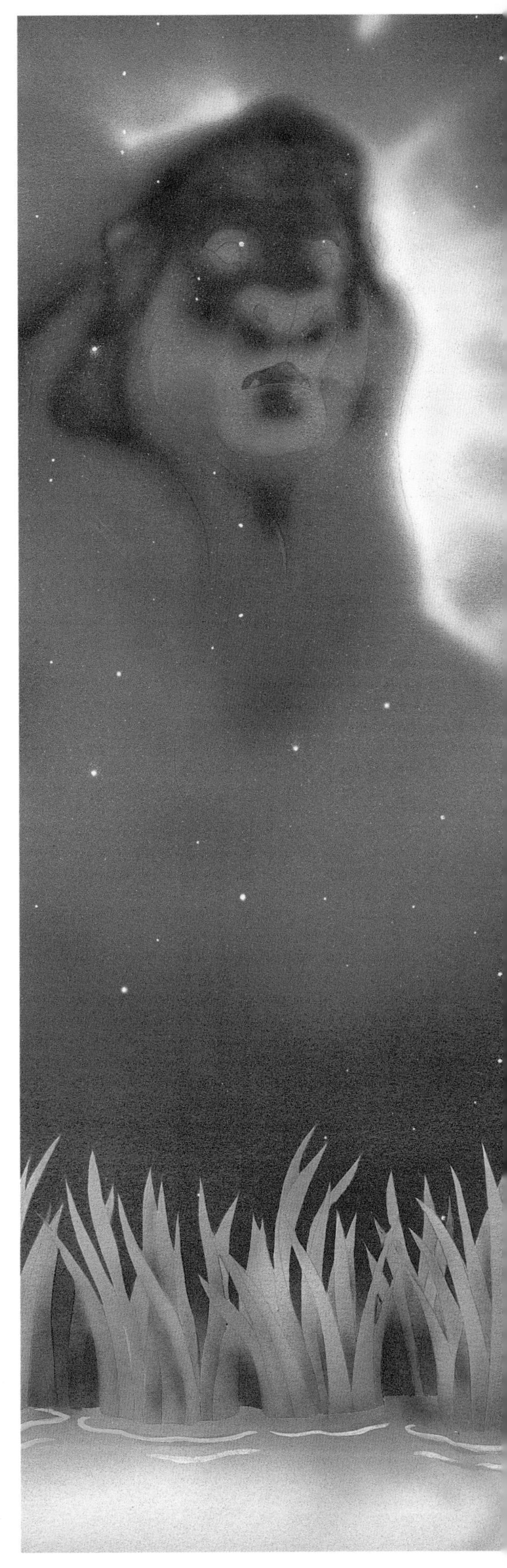

The reflection rose into the sky and Simba heard Mufasa's voice:

"Simba. You must take your place in the Circle of Life. You are my son and the one true King." Then the reflection and Rafiki disappeared.

Back at Pride Rock, the rains had been late coming and the land was dry. The hyenas paced impatiently round King Scar.

"We're starving," they howled. "The herds have gone. There's nothing left to eat."

Storm clouds gathered in the sky and a lightning bolt scorched the earth. As the dry grasses caught fire, flames swept towards Pride Rock. A lion appeared through the smoke. It was Simba!

Scar lunged at Simba, determined to kill him just as he had Mufasa. In the fierce battle that followed, Simba finally heaved Scar over the cliff face. Scar called to the hyenas to save him, but Nala and the lionesses drove them back. Simba was victorious!

Nala went to Simba's side. "Welcome home!" she whispered.

As they smiled at each other, it started to rain. The heavy drops soaked the dry ground and streambeds filled up once more. The plains came back to life and the herds returned.

One dawn the animals and birds made their way again to the foot of Pride Rock. Watched by the lions, Pumbaa and Timon, Rafiki picked up a tiny cub. He showed the new Prince – the son of King Simba and Queen Nala – to the cheering crowd below.

That night Simba watched the stars rise in the sky. “Everything’s all right, Father,” he said softly. “You see, I remembered.” And the stars seemed to twinkle in reply.

THE END

Disney
PRINCESS
Snow White
and the Seven Dwarfs

SNOW WHITE

THE PRINCE

STARRING

THE QUEEN

THE SEVEN DWARFS

Disney
PRINCESS
Snow White
and the Seven Dwarfs

Once upon a time, there lived a princess called Snow White. Snow White's father was dead, so she lived with her wicked stepmother, the Queen.

Snow White was very beautiful. Her skin was as white as snow, her hair as black as ebony wood, and her lips were as red as a red, red rose.

The Queen was also very beautiful but very vain. She had a magic mirror and every day she would look into it and say:

"Magic mirror on the wall,
Who is the fairest one of all?"

The mirror would always reply:
"You, O Queen, are the
fairest of them all."

But the Queen was still jealous of Snow White and made her work in the castle as a servant.

One day, after the Queen had spoken to her magic mirror, the mirror replied:

"Famed is thy beauty, Majesty,
But behold, a lovely maid I see.
Alas, she is more fair than thee,
Lips as red as a rose,
Hair as black as ebony,
Skin as white as snow."

The Queen was furious. "Snow White!" she hissed. "It cannot be!"

At that very moment, Snow White was singing beside the castle well.

A handsome prince, who was passing by, stopped to listen. As soon as the Prince and Snow White saw each other, they fell in love.

When the Queen saw Snow White with the Prince, she was furious and decided to get rid of her stepdaughter.

The next morning, the Queen told her huntsman to take Snow White into the forest and kill her. "Bring back her heart to prove she is dead," she ordered.

The Huntsman led the Princess into the forest but he could not kill her. He told Snow White to hide in the forest. Then he took an animal's heart to show the Queen that the Princess was dead.

Snow White wandered deep into the forest. She was very scared but the animals led her to a little cottage. Snow White knocked on the door and went inside. She wondered who could live in such a tiny house.

There were seven dusty little chairs at the table. In the sink there were seven dirty spoons and bowls. And in the bedroom there were seven unmade tiny beds.

"Perhaps untidy children live here," Snow White said.

So, with the help of her forest friends, Snow White dusted and cleaned the little cottage. Then she lay across three of the tiny beds and fell asleep.

Evening came and the owners of the cottage returned.

They were Seven Dwarfs, who worked in diamond mines, deep in the heart of the mountain. The Dwarfs marched along singing:

"Heigh-ho, heigh-ho,
It's home from work we go!"

As soon as they entered the cottage, they knew something was wrong – it was clean! The floor had been swept and there was a delicious smell coming from a pot on the fire.

"What's happened?" they asked each other in amazement.

They searched the cottage for an intruder. They reached the bedroom just as Snow White was waking up.

"Who are you?" they asked.

"My name is Snow White," said Snow White. She explained what she was doing there. Then she asked the little men who they were.

One by one, the Dwarfs introduced themselves.
"I'm Doc."
"I'm Grumpy."
"I'm Bashful."
"I'm Sleepy."
"I'm Sneezy."
"I'm Happy."
"And he's Dopey," they all shouted together.

"I'm very pleased to meet you all," said Snow White. "If you let me stay here, I promise I'll look after the house for you. I'll wash and sew and cook."

The Dwarfs quickly agreed!

That evening, the cottage was filled with music and laughter. The Dwarfs sang and danced to welcome the Princess to their home. Snow White was so happy that she soon forgot all about her wicked stepmother.

Meanwhile, back in the castle, the wicked stepmother said the special words to the magic mirror, and the mirror replied:

"Snow White, who dwells with the Seven Dwarfs,
Is as fair as you and as fair again."

The Queen was furious. "Snow White must still be alive!" she screamed. She vowed to get rid of Snow White once and for all.

Down in the dungeon, the Queen cast a magic spell to disguise herself as an old pedlar woman. Then, chanting a magic spell, she dipped a bright red apple into a pot of bubbling poison.

"One bite of this and Snow White will fall into a sleep as if dead," she cackled. "Only a kiss from her true love will wake her!"

The very next day, after the Dwarfs had left for work, the old pedlar woman called on Snow White selling apples.

"Try one, pretty maid," said the pedlar, handing Snow White an apple. "One bite and all your dreams will come true."

Snow White took one bite and fell to the floor as if dead.

"Now I'm the fairest in the land!" cried the wicked Queen, before fleeing.

Luckily, Snow White's forest friends had seen what had happened and went to fetch the Seven Dwarfs.

As the Dwarfs rushed towards the cottage, they spotted the Queen running away. They chased her through the forest and up the mountain.

The wicked Queen tried to roll a huge boulder on the dwarfs. But it rolled back and pushed her over the side of the mountain – never to be seen again.

When the Dwarfs returned to the cottage, they found Snow White lying on the floor as if she were dead. They could not wake her, so they took her into the forest. They placed her on a special bed and kept watch over her every day.

The months slowly passed. Snow White's bed was covered with leaves, then snow, and then the blossoms of spring.

She still did not wake up.

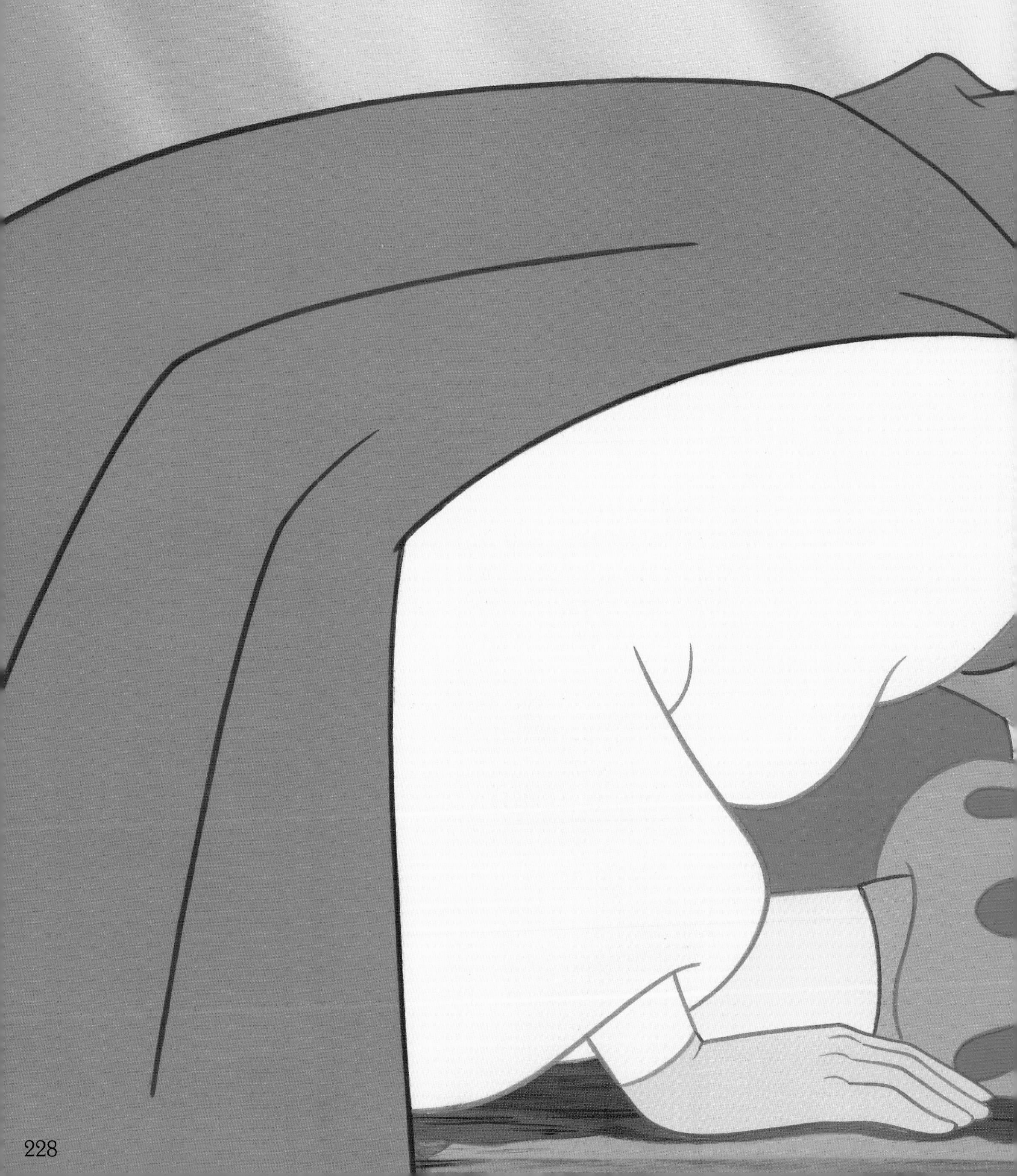

One day, a handsome young man came riding through the forest. He was the Prince who had fallen in love with Snow White by the castle well. When he saw the Princess, he got down from his horse, leant over her and kissed her.

All at once, Snow White's eyes fluttered open.

"She's awake!" the Dwarfs cried, excitedly. The wicked Queen's spell was broken.

Before Snow White left to begin her new life with the Prince, she kissed each of the Dwarfs. "I'll come and see you very soon," she promised them.

The Dwarfs watched the Prince lead Snow White away to her new life. They knew they would miss her but they also knew that she and the Prince would live happily ever after.

THE END

SPACE RANGER
LIGHTYEAR
LASER

WALL·E